THE SPECULATOR

A version of <u>Le Faiseur</u>
by
HONORE DE BALZAC

by
STEPHEN WYATT

Any enquiries regarding performance or reproduction
should be addressed to the author's agents:
Valerie Hoskins Associates,
20, Charlotte Street,
London W1P 1HJ
Telephone (020) 76374490

ISBN 978-0-95556868-4-9

INTRODUCTION

"Were I to die to-morrow, I should have more creditors
than relations inconsolable… The heart forgets, the crepe
wears out, but the unpaid debit is ineffaceable – the blank
is never filled up…"
(Translated by G.H. Lewes)

Le Faiseur is a comedy in which the financial wheeler-
dealer, Mercadet, contrives to stave off financial ruin by
various ruses, including marrying of his daughter to the
highest bidder and faking the return of his long-lost
business partner, who absconded eight years earlier with
most of their shared assets. The tone is more genial than
that of the novels of Balzac's Comédie Humaine but this
comedy of financial double-bluff still has a real edge to it
and seems all too relevant to our own crazy financial times.

The history of the piece is complicated. Honoré de Balzac
died in 1850 before the play was put into production. The
text was much altered by the playwright, Adolphe
d'Ennery, who reduced the five acts to three acts, dropped
several minor characters and substantially reworked parts
of the plot to give them a more conventionally theatrical
power. It was this version, first performed in 1851 with
considerable success, which went into the repertoire and,
was still being revived in Paris in the 1950s.

Meanwhile, in 1852, G.H. Lewes (under the pseudonym of
'Slingsby Lawrence') did an English version called The
Game of Speculation, which also enjoyed a number of
revivals during the nineteenth century. Lewes' adaptation is
closely based on the d'Ennery, with some further toning
down for English audiences – Mercadet becomes 'Affable
Hawk', the daughter's faithful young lover is called
'Noble' and at the end Hawk delivers a moralising speech
on the dangers of speculation.

The original five-act Balzac text, though published in his Collected Works, has, so far as I can tell, never been translated into English until I prepared this version for the Orange Tree. The original is less slick but much sharper in its observation and more psychologically complex in its treatment of the main characters.

In preparing my version, I've chosen a two act structure with Balzac's first and second acts played through as the first half and the other three acts forming the second half. I've also combined the two female servants of the original into one and sharpened or pruned Balzac's text where I felt it was necessary.

I am not, however, responsible for the naming of Mercadet's long-awaited business partner. It was Balzac who named him 'Godeau'. Indeed, both Eric Bentley and Martin Esslin believe this is the source for the name of the most famous unseen character in modern drama.

Stephen Wyatt

I am indebted to Peter Bonsall for help in preparing the initial literal translation of the text.

CHARACTERS:

AUGUSTE MERCADET. A speculator
ADOLPHE MINARD. A young bookkeeper.
MICHONNIN DE LA BRIVE. Young man about town.
DE MERICOURT. Another young man about town.
BREDIF. Mercadet's landlord
VERDELIN. Mercadet's friend.
BERCHUT. A broker.
GOULARD. A businessman. Mercadet's creditor.
PIERQUIN. A moneylender. Mercadet's creditor.
VIOLETTE. Mercadet's creditor.
JUSTIN. Mercadet's valet.

MADAME MERCADET.
JULIE MERCADET.
VIRGINIE. The Mercadets' housekeeper.

SETTING:
THE MAIN DRAWING ROOM OF MERCADET'S
APARTMENT. PARIS. 1839.

This version of Le Faiseur was commissioned by the
Orange Tree Theatre Richmond and was first performed on
the BBC World Service in 1997 in a production by Gordon
House with Martin Jarvis as Mercadet.

ACT ONE

MORNING.
BREDIF STANDS, SURVEYING
THE APARTMENT.

BREDIF: Just look at it - a superb apartment with eleven rooms right in the heart of Paris! And what's he paying for it? A measly two thousand five hundred francs a year! Ever since the July Revolution I've been losing three thousand francs - per annum. It's enough to make you ill. Never, ever complete a tenancy agreement while there's a revolution on. You'll live to regret it. Still, luckily Monsieur Mercadet is six quarters in arrears. The day can't be far off when I shall be rid of him. In the meantime, to tide me over, I shall grab what's left of the furniture. Better safe than -

MERCADET ENTERS DURING THIS.

MERCADET: So you're thinking of grabbing my furniture, are you? Up bright and early, I see, all ready to play havoc with the lives of your fellow men.

BREDIF: Forgive me, Monsieur Mercadet, but I can't really regard you as one of my fellows. I owe nothing, you are crippled with debts. I am in my own house, you are just a tenant.

MERCADET: So much for equality. Liberty and fraternity don't stand much chance either. Men will always be strictly

7

	divided into two classes - debtors and creditors. Don't you ever think -
BREDIF:	I'd rather think about my rent.
MERCADET:	I really don't understand you, Monsieur Brédif. You're the only one of my creditors who possesses some sort of security. Over the last eighteen months, you've been carefully removing my furniture piece by piece. That must be worth in all some fifty thousand francs - and I owe you for less than two years' rent. In any case, in a few months, I'll be able to -
BREDIF:	You seem to have forgotten about the interest I could have been earning on the money you owe me.
MERCADET:	That is a matter for the legal experts. All I can say is -
BREDIF:	My dear Monsieur, I'm not like you, a speculator. I live solely off the income from my properties. If all my tenants were like you... well, it doesn't bear thinking about.
MERCADET:	I just don't understand how you can contemplate throwing me out. You - who know all my sorrows. You - who know how hard I've laboured. You - who know how my confidence was cruelly abused by my partner, Godeau –
BREDIF:	Please don't start on that again. I know the sad story of his flight to the Indies. I've heard it many times - just like the rest of your creditors. Besides, I don't think you're fair to him. Godeau was a man of rare energy, a man who knew how to

	live. He lived with a most delightful woman -
MERCADET:	By whom he had a child. A child they both abandoned, don't forget.
BREDIF:	But it all turned out for the best, didn't it? His mother begged Monsieur Duval, your old cashier, to look after him. He was moved by her prayers and took charge of the young man -
MERCADET:	While Godeau took charge of our cashbox - one hundred and fifty thousand francs in all.
BREDIF:	Well, maybe he should have asked you first. But he left you all the other assets of the business, didn't he? And you've stayed in business, haven't you? For eight years you've been making huge profits. You've really prospered.
MERCADET:	Alas, all I've gained are Pyrrhic victories. That, it seems, is the lot of the speculator.
BREDIF:	But surely Godeau promised to give you half of what he made on his venture in the Indies? I'm sure he'll keep his word and come back.
MERCADET:	Well, if you're so sure, why not wait for him? He'll be able to pay you all that outstanding interest you talk about on top of what's owing in rent. Waiting for Godeau could be a sound investment.
BREDIF:	You have a point. But if landlords listened to their tenants, all they'd ever get is arguments of this sort. Besides, there's the government -
MERCADET:	What about the government?

BREDIF:	The government won't wait for its taxes. I'm afraid I have no choice but to proceed with the full rigour of the law and -
MERCADET	And I thought you were such a fine man! Don't you know that my daughter's about to get married? Can't you let the marriage go ahead? Why not come along yourself - bring your wife. I know she enjoys dancing. The day after the wedding we settle up.
BREDIF:	The day after the wedding is some way off. Today is somewhat nearer. My apologies if it scares off your son-in-law but you received a final demand the day before yesterday - and if you don't settle the debt today, the bankruptcy notices will be posted up tomorrow.
MERCADET:	So, tell me then, what do I have to offer you to gain myself another three months?
BREDIF:	A man with a strict conscience might hesitate to answer. After all, it would mean pulling the wool over the eyes of someone.
MERCADET:	Who exactly?
BREDIF:	Your future son-in-law.
MERCADET:	(ASIDE) Trust the old crook to spot that.
BREDIF:	Still, I'm a kind-hearted man. Surrender all your rights to the tenancy and I'll leave you in peace for three months.
MERCADET:	(ASIDE) Have you ever seen a piece of bread dropped in a fish-pond? I'm like that. Every fish wants a nibble. And my creditors are the pike. They

	won't stop nibbling till every crumb's eaten up. (ALOUD) Consider, we're in 1839. My lease has seven years to run. Rents have doubled -
BREDIF:	Thank goodness.
MERCADET:	But still in three months you'll turn me out - depriving my wife of the tenancy rights, the rights which will give her some protection if by any chance I -
BREDIF:	Go bankrupt.
MERCADET:	I'd really rather you didn't mention that word. Monsieur Brédif, do you know what drives even the honestest of debtors to subterfuge? It's his creditors - who bend the law to their thieving ends just to recover a few sous.
BREDIF:	Monsieur, I came here to be paid not insulted.
MERCADET:	You know, debt is punished far worse than crime. Commit a crime, at least you get a prison cell to lay your head in. Get into debt and you're thrown out on the streets. (PAUSE) Forgive me, monsieur. I'm at your mercy. I'll give up my tenancy rights.
BREDIF:	Monsieur, I don't want consent when it's given so grudgingly.
MERCADET:	You want me to thank you for what you're doing? (ASIDE) Better not provoke him too far. (ALOUD) I apologise if I've been too quick-tempered, Monsieur Brédif, but I am sorely tried. None of my creditors seem to appreciate how hard I am working in order to be able to pay them.

BREDIF:	In order to stay in business, you mean.
MERCADET:	But of course. Where would I be if I ever lost my right to attend the Bourse?

JUSTIN COMES IN - READY TO SHOW BREDIF OUT.

BREDIF:	Well then, let's finish this little business here and now.
MERCADET:	(ASIDE) Not in front of the servants, please. It's hard enough keeping the peace here as it is. Let's go downstairs to your apartment.
BREDIF:	(ASIDE) With any luck, in three months' time, I shall have this apartment back.

THEY LEAVE. JUSTIN IS LEFT ALONE. HE PULLS OUT A NEWSPAPER. THEN VIRGINIE ENTERS.

JUSTIN:	He's had a good run for his money, Virginie, but this time Monsieur Mercadet's going under. You can sometimes make a bit out of a master in debt but he owes me a year's wages now and something tells me it's time to go.
VIRGINIE:	These days when I go shopping, I have to pay for everything I buy. It's a real nuisance. You know, I've served in a number of respectable households but I've never come across one like this before. It's like something out of a play.

JUSTIN:	Yes - and we're having to do the acting. The performance you have to put on when a creditor turns up. "Oh, I'm sorry, monsieur, didn't you know? Monsieur Mercadet has left for Lyon - on business. Something to do with charcoal mines. It's looking very good, I gather." "So when will he be back?" "I really couldn't say, monsieur." Then there's the anxious version. "I'm sorry, monsieur, but it's poor Madame Mercadet. Monsieur and his daughter are in complete despair. They've taken her away to take the waters. We do fear that she may not be long for this world."
VIRGINIE:	I've got a much simpler way of getting rid of them. "You want to see Monsieur Mercadet? Well, I'm afraid he's out at present but if monsieur would like to see Mademoiselle Julie, she's in - and alone..." You can't see them for dust.
JUSTIN:	Poor Mademoiselle Julie, if only she were remotely pretty...
VIRGINIE:	Shall I tell you what I don't understand, Justin? What's the point of being a creditor? All you do is spend hours hanging around trying to catch Monsieur and when you do catch him, you spend even more hours listening to his excuses.
JUSTIN:	Well, they're all rich so it can't be that bad an occupation, can it?
VIRGINIE:	No, but they've given their money to Monsieur and he's not going to give it back, is he? It's like he's stolen it really.

JUSTIN:	Now, now, Virginie, be careful. If I take money out of your purse without your knowledge, well then, yes, I have stolen it. But if I say to you, "Virginie, I need a hundred sous, lend them to me please" and you give me the money and I don't pay you back then you have become my creditor. Understand?
VIRGINIE:	Not really. If I haven't got my money, it doesn't matter how I lost it, does it? (PAUSE) I'm going to ask for money to settle the housekeeping. The tradesmen won't give anything more without cash. And I'm not using my own money.
JUSTIN:	I've given Madame a number of broad hints about our wages but she doesn't seem to hear. I mean, are these people proper members of the bourgeoisie or aren't they? The bourgeoisie are supposed to spend freely on their housekeeping and take care of their servants - maybe even leave them a pension as a reward for faithful service. I can't see that happening here.
VIRGINIE:	Mind you, I'm not sure I want to leave till I know how it's all going to turn out. I've read all of Mademoiselle Julie's love letters secretly - and it's good fun teasing that little lover of hers, Minard. If there's a marriage, there are always perks. We ought to stay till the day after the wedding at least.
JUSTIN:	You don't seriously think Monsieur Mercadet is going to let his daughter

	marry a bookkeeper on eighteen hundred francs a year, do you?
VIRGINIE:	Why not? They're in love. (JUSTIN MAKES A FACE) Her mother's out every night and doesn't suspect a thing - but once Mademoiselle Julie's alone then little Minard turns up. They've haven't deigned to take me into their confidence so I feel it's only fair if I listen in on their conversation. Mademoiselle, you see, is like all plain women - she wants to be sure she's loved for herself. So she sits there working at her painting on porcelain while Minard reads her romantic novels. It's been going on like that for three months. When Madame comes home, Julie just says Minard dropped by to see her and since she was out, Julie received him on her mother's behalf.
JUSTIN:	So what sort of thing do the bourgeoisie say to each other when they're paying court?
VIRGINIE:	Oh, really silly things. They talk a lot about the ideal.
JUSTIN:	Nonsense, you mean. (PAUSE) Guess what Pere Grumeau told me.
VIRGINIE:	When?
JUSTIN:	Just now. He said that yesterday, when we were out shopping, two smart young men arrived in a cabriolet. According to their groom, one of them's going to marry Mademoiselle Mercadet. There must be something going on because Monsieur Mercadet slipped Pere Grumeau a hundred francs.

15

VIRGINIE:	A hundred francs - for the porter!
JUSTIN:	And what's more - in cash. Pere Grumeau was so impressed he kept telling the groom that Monsieur Mercadet had so much money that even he'd lost count of it.
VIRGINIE:	Now I think of it, I did see two young men leaving as I came back. They both had beautiful flowered waistcoats - and yellow gloves. And they were sitting in a coach pulled by a horse with a rose behind its ear - very classy. So one of them is going to marry Mademoiselle?
JUSTIN:	Apparently.
VIRGINIE:	Even though she's penniless - and has nothing in her favour except a nice singing voice?
JUSTIN:	You don't know Monsieur Mercadet. I've been with him for six years and I believe he's capable of anything - even getting rich again. There have been times when there have been writs plastered all over the door and I've thought he'd really had it this time - and still he bounces back. One day he'll go to bed ruined, the next day he'll wake up a millionaire. He never stops working. He's always drawing up prospectuses for new ventures designed to draw shareholders in like lambs to the slaughter. He floats companies in everything - from copper mines to paving stones, from laundries to silkworms. The only trouble is - however successful the latest enterprise, he still has his creditors on his back. It amazes me that he

16

manages to keep them at bay. I've seen them arriving, determined to seize everything and throw him in prison. He charms them, he makes them laugh, and they go away as if they were all still the best of friends. So maybe he can pull it off again after all. When you think of the people he's managed to keep sweet it's extraordinary. People like Pierquin -

VIRGINIE: That money-lending monster -

JUSTIN: Pere Violette -

VIRGINIE Poor old fool -

JUSTIN: And Goulard -

VIRGINIE: Who'd sell his own grandmother -

JUSTIN: Exactly. Besides, if -

VIRGINIE: Shush! Madame's coming. Maybe we'll hear some more about this marriage.

ENTER MADAME MERCADET, LOOKING CONCERNED.

MADAME: Justin, do you know where Monsieur Mercadet is?

JUSTIN: He went downstairs - with Monsieur Brédif.

MADAME: Ah, I see. (PAUSE) It's useless trying to hide from you my worries about my husband's business affairs. I hope we can rely on your discretion.

BOTH: Of course, Madame.

MADAME: Monsieur has great inner resources. He only needs time - so attend to his instructions carefully.

VIRGINIE: Madame, I would pass through fire for you. We were only just saying

17

	how lucky we were to have such good masters. If we stick by them in their troubles, we know they'll reward us handsomely when they're rich again.
JUSTIN:	As long as I have enough to scrape by on, I will serve monsieur. I am confident that on the day he brings off a successful business deal, we will all share in his prosperity.

MERCADET RETURNS BUT REMAINS, FOR THE MOMENT, UNNOTICED.

MADAME:	I'm confident you'll both be rewarded when Monsieur has his next financial triumph - which, I'm sure, will be very soon. In the meantime, however, we mustn't let our temporary embarrassment show. A rich suitor has presented himself for my daughter.
JUSTIN:	Mademoiselle Julie deserves to be happy - if I may be allowed to say so. She's so good, so refined -
VIRGINIE:	So talented - the voice of a nightingale.
JUSTIN:	It seems a pity that Mademoiselle is being denied the hats and dresses she so urgently needs. Perhaps, being ignorant of this match, the other servants haven't been handling the tradespeople as well as they might. I would be happy to take matters in hand. If Madame would care to give me the name of mademoiselle's suitor, I would be happy to visit all your suppliers and inform them that

	in case of difficulty they should refer to Monsieur... Monsieur?
MADAME:	De la Brive.
JUSTIN:	Monsieur de la Brive. Very good, Madame.
VIRGINIE:	Justin's right. If Madame had mentioned this match before, I would have told all the -
MADAME:	You can assure them they won't lose a centime by it.

MERCADET COMES FORWARD. HE TALKS SOFTLY TO HIS WIFE.

MERCADET:	Is this how you let the servants talk to you? You'll never keep their respect. (ALOUD) Justin, go at once to Monsieur Verdelin. Ask him to come here at once to discuss an urgent matter which simply won't brook delay. Tell him that if he can see his way to helping me out of my temporary difficulties it will be greatly to his advantage. Try to be as mysterious as you can. Just make sure he comes.

JUSTIN BOWS AND LEAVES.

MERCADET:	Well, Virginie, has Madame given you her orders yet?
VIRGINIE:	No, monsieur.
MERCADET:	Today, you must excel yourself. We have four people to dine - Verdelin and his wife, Monsieur de Méricourt and Monsieur de la Brive. Seven in all. This is your chance to display your culinary skills. So, after the

19

	soup, an exquisite fish, then four entrees finely prepared. Then, for the second course -
VIRGINIE:	But monsieur -
MERCADET:	What?
VIRGINIE:	The tradesmen.
MERCADET:	You talk to me about tradesmen on the day when my daughter is to meet her betrothed?
VIRGINIE:	I'm sorry, monsieur, but they'll refuse to give me anything.
MERCADET:	Then take my custom elsewhere.
VIRGINIE:	But how do I pay the ones I'm ditching?
MERCADET:	I wouldn't bother. That's their problem.
VIRGINIE:	But, monsieur, they might expect me to pay up personally. And I can't be held financially responsible.
MERCADET:	(ASIDE) This from a girl with a nice little nest egg put aside. (ALOUD) Virginie, today our very government relies on credit to keep going. If my tradesmen insist on payment and fail to acknowledge the fundamental principles on which their country is run then they are unpatriotic scoundrels. I don't choose to waste my time thinking about such ignoramuses. And you - just concentrate on showing what you are - a true cordon bleu. If by any chance, the day after my daughter's marriage, Madame Mercadet finds she's in your debt, then, of course, I will be answerable for everything.
VIRGINIE:	But, monsieur -
MERCADET:	Enough! You know, Virginie, those savings of yours -

VIRGINIE:	What about them, monsieur?
MERCADET:	I could help you to get a return of ten francs per hundred francs every half year. What does that saving bank of yours offer?
VIRGINIE:	Barely ten sous a year.
MERCADET:	As little as that! And for a return like that, you entrust your hard-earned money to complete strangers? I'm shocked. I'm sure you're bright enough to take up my suggestion instead. That way you'll make your money really work for you - and be able to keep an eye on it at the same time.
VIRGINIE:	(ASIDE) Ten francs every six months! It does sound good. (ALOUD) As for the second course, monsieur, Madame can tell me later. I'll go and prepare the luncheon.

EXIT VIRGINIE.

MERCADET:	That girl has three thousand francs in a saving bank which she's systematically stolen from us. At least now we've got a chance of recouping some of our money.
MADAME:	Oh, Auguste, how low are you prepared to stoop?
MERCADET:	As low as necessary, my dear. Besides, it's all very well for you to criticise - out every night enjoying yourself at the theatre or some smart gathering with our friend, Méricourt -
MADAME:	But you asked me to go out with him.

MERCADET:	You know perfectly well that I'm too busy. And very fine and elegant you look too.
MADAME:	Again - on your instructions.
MERCADET:	Of course. It's essential for you to look good. Every speculator needs a woman to carry the flag. When you appear at the Opera in some splendid new outfit, then everybody says, "Madame Mercadet is looking very chic. Asphalt's must be doing well." Or - "She's positively radiant. The Family Provident's gone up."
MADAME:	And all the time I'm worrying about the desperate plight you're in.
MERCADET:	Then please don't criticise the means I'm using to get myself out of it. Just now with the servants - you were practically pleading with them. You must take command - just as Napoleon did.
MADAME:	But ordering things we can't pay for -
MERCADET:	Exactly. Nothing succeeds like excess.
MADAME:	But surely there's still a place for loyalty - and affection -
MERCADET:	Loyalty! Affection! My dear, what sort of age do you think you're living in? Today sentiment's out the window, money is the sole motivation. Today there aren't families any longer, just individuals, all ruled by self-interest and thoughts of future profit. A daughter's main concern is to see her dowry's properly invested and her husband's is to grab it for his own ends. A wife's main means of support isn't her husband but the local savings

	bank - and everyone's idea of paying their debt to their country is to grab all they can. No wonder servants change as fast as the map of Europe.
MADAME:	I hate hearing you talk like this.
MERCADET:	You mean it's only a short step from thinking it to doing it?
MADAME:	You've always been so honest, so honourable -
MERCADET:	Well, let me tell you something, my dear. I shall do all that's necessary to save myself because this is modern honour. (HE PULLS OUT A FIVE FRANC PIECE) You could start off by selling plaster off as sugar, any cheap swindle, and as long as you manage to get rich without being caught out, you could end up as a deputy, a peer - even a minister. Why are thieving rascals so popular on the stage? Because the audience all sit there smugly congratulating themselves on being so much smarter. At least I have an excuse - Godeau's crime. Not that I consider there's anything particularly shameful about being in debt. Name me a single country in Europe that isn't. Besides, life is one long loan. Every man owes his very being to his parents and he'll be dead before he can pay that back. Even the very earth is perpetually in debt to the sun that shines upon it. In any case, am I not superior to my creditors? I have their money, they wait for mine. I ask nothing from them, they constantly beg from me. If a man owes nothing then nobody gives him

	a thought - whereas my creditors are obsessed with me.
MADAME:	But owing and paying back is one thing. Owing and not paying back, borrowing what you know you can't repay, is another.
MERCADET:	You don't approve?
MADAME:	It worries me sick.
MERCADET:	Then you no longer trust me.
MADAME:	Oh, I'll always trust you - but I despair when I see you wearing yourself out to so little effect. The brilliance of your plans is beyond doubt, my dear, but it worries me when you try to delude yourself about your chances of success with all this shallow wit.
MERCADET:	If I didn't keep my spirits up, my dear, I would have gone under already. Acres of regret won't pay back a sous of debt. Can you honestly tell me where probity begins and ends in the commercial world? It's not as clear as you think. You know we have no capital.
MADAME:	That much I'd gathered.
MERCADET:	Well, then, what do we do? Nobody will give us a sou if they know that, will they? So please don't condemn the means I'm using to keep my place in the uncertain world of speculation. You can't obtain credit without deception. When you go out each night wearing magnificent jewellery, you're helping me far more than you know. Plenty have behaved far worse. Even Louis XIV had to show off his palaces to screw money out of the financiers.

MADAME:	My dear, you don't have to justify yourself to me any more. So long as you behave honourably -
MERCADET:	You may feel sorry for our creditors but you know perfectly well we can only hold on to their money while they believe that -
MADAME:	We are to be trusted?
MERCADET:	No, that they can still make a profit out of us. The speculator and the shareholder share the same dream. They both want instant wealth. In the past, I've helped all my creditors to make a killing and all of them still believe I might be able to do the same in the future. That's where my intimate knowledge of their characters comes in handy. I play along with each of them, adapting my performance as necessary.
MADAME:	I'm still worried about the outcome. Some of them have lost all patience - Goulard for one. He'll show no mercy. He's determined to make you file for bankruptcy.
MERCADET:	Never while there's breath in my body! Never till the gold mines of Mexico move to Paris! I will never give in - until I am rich again.

ENTER GOULARD.

GOULARD:	Ah, there you are, my dear monsieur.
MADAME:	(WARNING HIM) Auguste, it's Goulard.

MERCADET INDICATES FOR HER TO BE CALM.

GOULARD:	It seems you have to be up early to find a time when the doors are open and the keepers absent!
MERCADET:	Keepers? Are we beasts in the Zoo? Goulard, you are priceless -
GOULARD:	No, simply unpaid. And I'm not going to be satisfied with words.
MERCADET:	Of course not. You need deeds. What sort of payment do you have in mind? I can offer shares in -
GOULARD:	Let us not fool around. I've come to put an end to all that.
MADAME:	An end, Monsieur Goulard?
MERCADET:	Be calm, my dear. Let Monsieur Goulard speak.
GOULARD:	As a matter of fact, Madame, I'm glad you're here. Your signature could -
MERCADET:	Please don't involve my wife. She knows nothing about business. (TO MADAME) Monsieur, my dear, is my creditor. He's come here to demand the settlement of his debt in cash along with the interest and expenses attached. But he's not behaving in a reasonable manner. He's pursuing a man with whom in the past he's often done business.
GOULARD:	Business that hasn't always worked to my advantage.
MERCADET:	What do you expect? If business always worked to your advantage, everybody would be doing it.
GOULARD:	I've not come here to collect samples of your wit. I've come here because you have my money.

MERCADET:	Well, somebody has to have it. (TO MADAME) You see here a man who's been pursuing me like a bloodhound. Come, Goulard, let's agree that you've been behaving very badly. Anybody but myself would be sorely tempted to get his own back. Particularly as it's in my power to make you lose a very considerable sum.
GOULARD:	By not paying me, you mean? Well, you are going to pay me - or else tomorrow I call in the bailiffs.
MERCADET:	Oh, I'm not talking about that. You needn't have any worries about what I owe you. I'm talking about a considerably larger amount of money than that. I'm really surprised that a shrewd man like yourself, a man whose judgement I respect, is still tied up in the whole sad business. But I suppose we all make mistakes.
GOULARD:	I don't follow.
MERCADET:	(TO MADAME) You wouldn't credit it, would you, my dear? (TO GOULARD) She's become quite an expert over the years, you know. She has developed a real instinct for judging the markets. (TO MADAME) Well, my dear, it looks as if Goulard is still in for a large sum.
MADAME:	(BAFFLED) Monsieur -
GOULARD:	(ASIDE) Mercadet really knows the markets, that's for sure. Or is he just playing games with me?

	(ALOUD) My dear Mercadet, what are you talking about? I really don't understand.
MERCADET:	Oh, I think you do. When it comes to shares, you can always tell where the shoe pinches - isn't that the phrase?
GOULARD:	You can't mean the Lower Indre mines, can you? Surely that's a wonderful investment.
MERCADET:	Oh, absolutely - for those who sold their shares yesterday.
GOULARD:	You sold...?
MERCADET:	In secret, of course, on the outer ring. You'll see the fall today and tomorrow. And, of course, tomorrow, when the truth about the whole business finally comes out...

GOULARD STARTS TO LEAVE.

GOULARD:	My thanks, Mercadet. We'll talk of our little business later. Madame, my respects.
MERCADET:	(TAKING HIS ARM) Just a moment. I've another piece of news which should set your mind at rest.
GOULARD:	What about?
MERCADET:	About what I owe you. My daughter's getting married.
GOULARD:	(TRYING TO LEAVE) Later.
MERCADET:	What's the hurry? She's marrying a millionaire.
GOULARD:	My congratulations. I hope she'll be very happy. You can count on me.

MADAME:	For the wedding, you mean?
GOULARD:	Whenever.
MERCADET:	(STOPPING HIM AGAIN) One more thing -
GOULARD:	No, goodbye. I wish you every success.
MERCADET:	If you pushed a few of your securities my way, I could advise you on whom to sell your shares to.
GOULARD:	Dear Mercadet, we're going to settle up later.
MERCADET:	(TO MADAME) He can't wait to put one over on his fellow men.
GOULARD:	Is that all?
MERCADET:	Didn't you bring all the documents with you?
GOULARD:	No.
MERCADET:	Then why did you come?
GOULARD:	I came to see how you were getting on.
MERCADET:	I'm touched. We're as you see.
GOULARD:	I'm delighted. Adieu.

HE FINALLY BREAKS FREE
AND HURRIES OUT.

MERCADET:	(LAUGHING) There's no holding him back.
MADAME:	(ALSO LAUGHING) But is what you told him true? I honestly can't tell any more.
MERCADET:	Well, put it like this. It's is in the interests of my friend, Verdelin, to organise a run on shares in the Lower Indre mines. Up to now the whole enterprise has been looking distinctly unpromising but it's suddenly going to take off

and before it does, Verdelin wants to buy up all the shares cheaply. (ASIDE) So if Goulard does start a panic, I've played my part. (ALOUD) But let's turn to our own great enterprise - Julie's marriage. Really, you know, I need a second self to keep track of everything that's happening.

MADAME: If you'd only let me be your cashier, today we'd be receiving thirty thousand francs a year in rents.

MERCADET: The day I have thirty thousand francs in rents is the day I'll be ruined. Just think, if we'd buried ourselves away in the provinces, as you wanted, with the little we had left over after Godeau had helped himself, where would we be now? For a start, you'd never have got to know Méricourt. He's a perfect companion for you and he's the means by which we'll get Julie off our hands. Let us be frank, my dear, the poor girl is not the most beautiful example of God's handiwork.

MADAME: There are sensible men who think beauty fades.

MERCADET: And there are plenty more who think plainness lasts.

MADAME: Julie is very loving.

MERCADET: Indeed, but I'm not Monsieur de la Brive and I know a father's role in all this. I'm concerned about the sudden passion this young man has conceived for my

	daughter. I'd like to know what charmed him about her.
MADAME:	Julie has a lovely voice. She's very musical.
MERCADET:	Maybe he's a music lover then. All the same -
MADAME:	Julie is also well-educated.
MERCADET:	She reads novels, you mean. At least she has the good sense not to write them. I just hope she hasn't been so affected by her reading that she fails to appreciate that marriage is not a matter of affection but a matter of business. We've left her to her own devices far too much this last couple of years. She has grand ideas.
MADAME:	The poor child knows enough about our difficulties to try and learn a skill. She's learned how to paint on porcelain - so as not to be a burden to us.
MERCADET:	Pity she didn't learn how to be beautiful.
MADAME:	She's better than that. She's virtuous.
MERCADET:	Romantic and virtuous. I'm sure her husband will consider those admirable selling points. Go and find her. She needs to know the purpose of tonight's dinner - and to be prepared to take Monsieur de la Brive's approaches seriously.
MADAME:	I meant to talk to her yesterday but there was all that trouble with the tradesmen. I'll fetch her. She's bound to be up. She always gets

up at dawn now to start on her painting.

EXIT MADAME MERCADET.

MERCADET: In times like these it's hard enough marrying off a daughter who's young and beautiful. When she's plain, with only her virtue as dowry, I defy the most scheming of mothers to bring it off. Still, Méricourt seems fond of us. He and my wife have hit it off. So, hopefully, he feels obliged to help Julie to an advantageous marriage. As for Monsieur de la Brive, well, the most demanding parent would be impressed by the sight of him sitting in his box at the Opera or whipping his horse along the Champs Elysees. What's more, I've dined at his place - a most charming apartment. The silver was excellent and the dinner service had his coat of arms on it so it can't have been borrowed. But I can't help wondering why such a fashionable young man wants to get married. Perhaps he's bored with his successes with women and wants to settle down. According to Méricourt, he heard Julie singing at the Duvals' and was enchanted. Not the strongest foundation for a marriage but there have been worse.

MME. MERCADET COMES
BACK WITH JULIE.

MADAME:	Julie, your father and I have to speak to you on a subject close to a girl's heart. Somebody has presented himself as your suitor. It's possible that you'll soon be married, my child.
JULIE:	Possible? Isn't it certain?
MERCADET:	Eligible girls have no doubts on the subject apparently!
JULIE:	Has Monsieur Minard spoken to you then, father?
MERCADET:	Monsieur Minard? What about him? (PAUSE) Tell me, Madame, did you expect to find a Monsieur Minard already occupying a special place in your daughter's heart? Julie, is this by any chance that little book-keeper that Duval has several times recommended to me for jobs? A poor lad, the offspring of an unmarried mother and a crook called Godeau? Answer me.
JULIE:	Yes, father.
MERCADET:	You love him?
JULIE:	Yes, father.
MERCADET:	It's all very well loving, you need to be loved as well.
MADAME:	Does he love you?
JULIE:	Oh yes, mother.
MERCADET:	Yes, mother, yes, father. When girls have grown up, they shouldn't still be talking as if they've just left the wet nurse. Do your mother the courtesy of calling her 'Madame'.

JULIE:	Yes, monsieur.
MERCADET:	'Father' is quite sufficient for me. Now, what proofs do you have of being loved?
JULIE:	I feel loved.
MERCADET:	Anything more tangible?
JULIE:	The best proof of all - he wants to marry me.
MERCADET:	I think I'm going crazy.
MADAME:	Where did you see him?
JULIE:	Here.
MADAME:	When?
JULIE:	In the evening when you were out.
MADAME:	He's younger than you.
JULIE:	It's only a matter of months.
MADAME:	I believed you had more sense than to think of a stupid young man of twenty-eight who can't possibly appreciate your qualities.
JULIE:	But he thought of me first. Because if I'd fallen in love first, he would never have known. We met one evening at Madame Grandet's.
MADAME:	Only Madame Grandet would think of receiving people without proper social standing!
MERCADET:	I'm afraid she sees herself as a hostess and she'll take dancing partners at any price. Men who dance never have any future. Ambitious young men today put on a serious air and never go near the dance floor.
JULIE:	But Adolphe -
MERCADET:	Oh, it's Adolphe now, is it? that's all we need. Idiots keep on assuring us the world is making

progress but it's quite clearly gone into reverse. Children pay no attention whatsoever to the hard-earned experience of their parents. Well, do try and understand if you can. mademoiselle. An employee on eighteen hundred francs a year doesn't know how to love. He's too busy working. It's only the idle rich, with nothing better to do, who can afford to fall in love.

MADAME: You misguided child, don't you -

MERCADET: Let me speak to her please, my dear. Julie, supposing I let you marry your Monsieur Minard - no, let me finish. You won't have a sou to your name so what'll become of you once you're married? Have you thought about that?

JULIE: Yes, father.

MADAME: She's crazy.

MERCADET: She's in love, which is far worse. Come on now, Julie, think of me not as your father but your confidant. How will you manage? I'm all attention.

JULIE: We will love each other.

MERCADET: And trust to Cupid to provide the rent money?

JULIE: Oh, father, you don't understand. If we have to, we'll go and live in a small apartment, far away, somewhere in the suburbs - on the fourth floor if necessary. We won't need a servant - I'll happily do all the household chores because I'll be doing them for

35

him. I'll work hard for him and he'll be out working hard for me. Just because we're poor doesn't mean that our dwelling can't be clean - elegant even. After all, elegance reflects inner contentment and we'll be content. Besides, I'll earn enough with my painting to cost Adolphe nothing. I'll even be able to contribute towards our living costs. If times do get hard then love will see us through. Adolphe has an elevated soul and I know he has it in him to succeed.

MERCADET: He may be young and hopeful now but a few years of trying to earn enough to live on will put pay to that.

JULIE: Father, Adolphe has both determination and ability. I'm sure if he set his mind to it, he could become anything - even a cabinet minister.

MERCADET: Everybody these days thinks they can become a cabinet minister, Fresh out of school, everybody is convinced they're going to be great poets or great orators - or great ministers. Just the same as under the Empire, every new sub-lieutenant thought he'd follow in Napoleon's shoes. Shall I tell you what will happen to your precious Adolphe? He'll father a brood of children who will upset all your careful plans, dump his excellency in the debtors' prison and leave you looking after them.

	(TO MADAME) I've rarely seen the dangers of romantic fiction so clearly illustrated.
MADAME:	Poor child, at her age it's easy to confuse hopes with realities.
MERCADET:	She appears to believe that love is the only ingredient needed for a happy marriage. She'll be like all the others. When it goes wrong, she'll blame the very society whose rules she's deliberately flouting. Luckily, this is only a passing infatuation, nothing serious.
JULIE:	Ours is a love for which we'll sacrifice everything.
MADAME:	What, even your father? Julie, you don't know what you're saying. You have it in your power to restore to him our family honour, something even more precious than the life we gave you.
MERCADET:	Indeed. What's the point of devouring all those novels if you're not prepared to make the sort of heroic sacrifices they recommend? Does your Adolphe know the true state of your fortune? Have you painted him that delightful Rousseauesque picture of life on the fourth floor with nothing but a bowl of cherries for sustenance?
JULIE:	Father, you know I'd never commit the least indiscretion that might compromise you.
MERCADET:	So he still thinks we're rich?

JULIE:	He's never spoken to me of money.
MERCADET:	Better and better... Julie, you must go at once and tell him to come and have a talk with me.
JULIE:	(EMBRACING HIM) Thank you, father.
MERCADET:	I must, however, also tell you that this very day another young man is dining here - an elegant young man with a good name and exalted social position who also has intentions towards you. He is my choice for you. You are to be - not Madame Minard - but Madame de la Brive. Instead of your picturesque garret, you'll live in a grand house on the Chausée d'Antin. With your talent and education, you will then be able to play a brilliant role in Parisian society. If you don't become the wife of a minister, you will at least become the wife of a peer of France. I'm sorry, my dear, that I don't have anything better to offer.
JULIE:	Don't laugh at my love, please, father. Allow me to prefer happiness and poverty to wealth and misery.
JULIE:	Julie, your father and I are responsible for your future whether it suits you or not. We don't want to be accused later on of not having fulfilled our obligations to you. You are about to learn a harsh but valuable lesson in the ways of the world.

	You must go and marry wealth. If you're poor and miserable, there's nothing to be done. If you're rich and miserable, at least you can go out and spend money to make yourself feel better.
JULIE:	Mother, I can't believe you're saying such things to me. And, father, since you've been frank with me, I hope I can be frank with you. Haven't I heard you talk about rich people and how miserable they are in their idleness? Haven't you said that, in order to compensate for their unhappiness, they fall into self-indulgent vices that destroy their families? Isn't it better to let your daughter marry a man who may lack riches now but is at least capable of earning them? Monsieur de la Brive may well be wealthy, talented and witty but so were you when you married my mother - and she was rich and beautiful. You've still lost all your money.
MERCADET:	Julie, you're free to judge Monsieur de la Brive every bit as harshly as I judge Monsieur Minard. But in the end, you won't have a choice. Monsieur Minard will give you up himself.
JULIE:	Never! He'll win you over.
MADAME:	Maybe if she is loved -
MERCADET:	I think she's mistaken.
JULIE:	If I am mistaken, then all I ask is to be always so.

THE DOOR BELL RINGS.

MADAME:	Someone's ringing - and none of the servants are here to answer.
MERCADET:	Let it ring.
MADAME:	I always think - maybe Godeau's come back.
MERCADET:	Godeau! With his talent for making money, he probably got hung from the yard arm of a pirate ship before he even reached the Indies. After eight years without news, you're still hoping Godeau will turn up! You're like all those old soldiers waiting for the return of Napoleon.
MADAME:	They're still ringing.
MERCADET:	It sounds like a creditor's ring to me. Go and see, Julie. And whatever they say to you, tell them your mother and I are out. If this creditor has any decency left, he'll believe an innocent young girl like yourself.

EXIT JULIE.

MADAME:	This love of hers worries me.
MERCADET:	You're both romantics.
MADAME:	But there's such power in a first love.
MERCADET:	Only the power to drive them into debt. And there's enough of that around already with the bride's father.

JULIE RETURNS WITH PIERQUIN.

40

JULIE:	It's Monsieur Pierquin, father.
MERCADET:	The young guard's been outwitted then.
JULIE:	He said it concerned a good business deal for you.
MERCADET:	For himself he means! (TO MADAME) I can just about understand her trusting that precious Adolphe of hers - but to believe a creditor! Still, I know how to handle this one. Leave us.

MADAME MERCADET GOES OUT WITH JULIE.

PIERQUIN:	I've not come here to ask you for money, my dear monsieur. I've heard you've made a superb marriage for your daughter. She's to marry a millionaire. News spreads fast.
MERCADET:	Maybe not a millionaire, Pierquin. But he does have certain assets...
PIERQUIN:	Exactly. This magnificent prospect will calm your creditors. For my own part, I've recalled all the legal documents I'd sent to the bailiffs.
MERCADET:	You were going to have me arrested!
PIERQUIN:	You've had two years to repay the loans. I've never kept anybody on the files that long. For you, I've broken all the rules. If this marriage is just an invention then I congratulate you. Godeau's return has always been a clever card to play and a son-in-law should gain your further time.

41

	You've lead us all a merry dance, my dear monsieur. I admire your nerve. And to marry off a daughter without a dowry to a rich husband, real or not - well, it's a masterstroke.
MERCADET:	(ASIDE) He's leading up to something.
PIERQUIN:	Goulard's swallowed it all, hook, line and sinker. What I'd like to know is - what's the catch? I'm sure it's an ingenious one.
MERCADET:	My future son-in-law is Monsieur de la Brive, a young man -
PIERQUIN:	You mean, there really is a young man?
MERCADET:	I'll show him to you.
PIERQUIN:	So how much are you paying him?
MERCADET:	That's quite enough insolence from you, thank you, Pierquin. Otherwise, I shall be forced to ask you to settle our accounts. And, if we do settle, you stand to lose a great deal on the price you lent me the money at.
PIERQUIN:	Monsieur -
MERCADET:	Soon I shall again be rich enough not to have to endure the gibes of anyone - not even one of my creditors. So what business proposal exactly have you come to me with?
PIERQUIN:	If you really want to settle, I'll be happy to do so.
MERCADET:	I very much doubt it. I bring you a bigger yield than a huge farm in Provence.

PIERQUIN:	Well, then, I've come to offer you a set of promissory notes. If you take them over then I'll grant you a stay of three months.
MERCADET:	And that's the good deal?
PIERQUIN:	Yes.
MERCADET:	(ASIDE) What's the old fox after? The goose with the golden eggs? (ALOUD) Explain yourself more precisely.
PIERQUIN:	You know me, Mercadet. Down to earth, transparently honest, full of -
MERCADET:	Spare me the testimonials. I've never reproached you with being a money-lender. A high interest rate is an unavoidable necessity when you're raising capital for a business. A moneylender is simply a capitalist who plays his part in advance.
PIERQUIN:	(PRODUCING PAPERS) Here are nearly fifty thousand francs in letters of exchange belonging to a handsome young man called Michonnin, an easy-going lad -
MERCADET:	Who's not going any further?
PIERQUIN:	Exactly. Look, everything's in order. First Application. Provisional Judgement. Final Judgement. Hearing of Bankruptcy. Proclamation of Seizure etc etc. There are also five thousand francs outstanding in expenses.
MERCADET:	You're trying to tell me this is worth something?
PIERQUIN:	It's worth exactly as much as the future prospects of the young man

	- who'll have to work hard in order to survive.
MERCADET:	Worthless, you mean.
PIERQUIN:	Not if he manages to marry this young Englishwoman who's in love with -
MERCADET:	Him?
PIERQUIN:	No, with a title. I did think of buying him one but I haven't got the time to waste on greasing the right palms.
MERCADET:	So what exactly do you want from me in return for this magnificent offer?
PIERQUIN:	Something of real value.
MERCADET:	I don't follow.
PIERQUIN:	I want your old shares - all the old ones that don't pay dividends any more.
MERCADET:	And for that you'll give me a stay of five months?
PIERQUIN:	<u>Three</u> months.
MERCADET:	(ASIDE) Three months! That's an eternity in the life of a speculator. Anything could happen. But what's Pierquin's game? Still, if the shares are worthless, what have I to lose? (ALOUD) Pierquin, I'm not sure I fully understand but I agree.
PIERQUIN:	I had counted on that. (TAKING DOCUMENTS FROM HIS FOLDER) Here's a letter by which I accord you a stay of proceedings. And here are the documents relating to Michonnin. I ought to warn you. This young man's successfully lead all the bailiffs by the nose.

MERCADET:	(SEARCHING FOR HIS OWN FOLDER) So what would you like from me? I've some red shares here relating to a newspaper which could be very successful if it ever appeared. Or how about some blue shares for a mine which has already gone up in smoke? Then there are these yellow ones -
PIERQUIN:	Give me all colours.
MERCADET:	Yours for fifty thousand francs.
PIERQUIN:	(TAKING THEM) Thank you, my dear friend. People like us always play fair and square, eh?
MERCADET:	(ASIDE) He always said that when he's screwed someone. I must have been robbed. (ALOUD) You're going to pass these shares on then, I presume?
PIERQUIN:	Of course.
MERCADET:	For what they're nominally worth?
PIERQUIN:	If at all possible.
MERCADET:	Ah, now I understand. They're going to replace those musty furs, ivory carvings and all the rest of that old junk you force people to accept instead of ready cash.
PIERQUIN:	That's old-fashioned now.
MERCADET:	And the law doesn't like it much either, does it? So you're going to breathe new life into these shares and make people accept them as loans instead - and at face value.
PIERQUIN:	I'll do my best. In the meantime, in my role of creditor, I wish you every success in the business of your daughter's marriage. Farewell.

HE LEAVES. MERCADET
THUMBS THROUGH THE
FOLDER OF PAPERS.

MERCADET: Michonnin, forty two thousand. Plus five thousand in interest and expenses. Forty seven thousand in all. Some hope! Still a man who's worth nothing today may become credit-worthy tomorrow. Maybe I should get him made a baron and marry him off... Just a moment, my wife knows a rich Englishwoman who might do - the daughter of a brewer, appalling dress sense... Damn, it says here: No fixed abode. That does for it. But then who am I to cast the first stone? I may very well be of no fixed abode myself in three months' time. Poor lad, perhaps he had a Godeau too - a false friend who betrayed him. But no, I mustn't be unjust. If I'm honest, Godeau's been a good investment. He's already brought me in more money than he took from me.

HE STUDIES THE PAPERS
FURTHER THEN RINGS.
JUSTIN ENTERS FOLLOWED BY
VIRGINIE.

MERCADET: So what did my friend, Verdelin say, Justin?

JUSTIN: He's going to come. He hinted he might just about be able to scrape together enough money to settle Monsieur Brédif for you.

MERCADET:	Did he? Well, make sure he speaks to me before he speaks to my landlord. Just a moment - I gave the porter a hundred francs, didn't I? He hasn't lied on my behalf in the last twenty four hours.
JUSTIN:	Especially since I convinced him he was telling Monsieur de la Brive's groom the truth.
MERCADET:	You'll end up as my secretary, Justin.
JUSTIN:	I thought secretaries had to write.
MERCADET:	Not if they're secretaries to cabinet ministers, they don't. Their main function is to keep on talking when the minister can't open his mouth without incriminating himself. So go and make sure that old porter tells Verdelin that Monsieur Brédif is out.

JUSTIN GOES.

MERCADET:	Well, Virginie, how's supper coming along?
VIRGINIE:	As soon as I promised payment, they were most obliging.
MERCADET:	I thought they would be. So everything's in order for tonight?
VIRGINIE:	Yes, monsieur.
MERCADET:	And the tradesmen?
VIRGINIE:	They'll wait.
MERCADET:	(ASIDE) Excellent! She's paid them herself. (ALOUD) I won't forget this Virginie. We'll settle tomorrow.
VIRGINIE:	When mademoiselle marries, no doubt she'll bear me in mind.
MERCADET:	Of course.

VIRGINIE GOES.

MERCADET: You need to have your servants on your side - the same way a minister needs the support of the press. Luckily, mine have their wages at stake. Everything now depends on the dubious support of my friend, Verdelin, a man whom I have made rich. But what's the point in condemning ingratitude? Everyone over forty knows the world's full of it. In any case, Verdelin and I are even. I owe him money, he owes me gratitude - and neither of us pays up. However, in order to marry Julie, I need a thousand écus from the pocket of a man who's always claiming it's empty. It's going to be hard to persuade him to part with his cash. Only a woman who's got a man besotted with her can bring off miracles like that.

JUSTIN: (ENTERING) Monsieur Verdelin's on his way.

BUT IT'S PERE VIOLETTE WHO COMES IN.

MERCADET: My dear friend - (STOPPING) Ah, it's Pere Violette, good to see you. (TO JUSTIN) How many times have I told you to keep the doors shut so people can't just walk in? Go and keep an eye out for Verdelin - then keep him entertained until I've got rid of this poor devil.

JUSTIN: (ASIDE) Another one of his victims!

VIOLETTE:	I've already been here eleven times in eight days, dear Monsieur Mercadet. Yesterday I waited for three hours out in the street to try and catch you on your way back from the Bourse. But I gather you've been away in the country.
MERCADET:	Ah, my poor Pere Violette, we're as unfortunate as each other. We both have families to look after.
VIOLETTE:	We've pawned everything we can.
MERCADET:	Same here.
VIOLETTE:	But at least you still have enough to live on. We're without bread. I've never reproached you with my ruin because I believe you genuinely wanted to make us rich. It's my own fault as well. In trying to double our little fortune, I put everything at risk. My wife and children don't try to understand what's happened. Even though they kept on at me to take the risk, telling me I was being too timid and nothing ventured, nothing gained... But enough, talking doesn't pay the bills. I've come to beg you to give me just a little on account of what's owing. You'll save the life of a whole family.
MERCADET:	(ASIDE) Poor man, he breaks my heart. The sight of him quite takes my appetite away. (ALOUD) Stay calm, Violette, I'm going to deal plainly with you. (SOTTOVOCE) We've scarcely one hundred francs in the house - and that's my daughter's money.
VIOLETTE:	It can't be true! You've always appeared so rich.

49

MERCADET:	As one unfortunate to another, I feel I owe you the truth.
VIOLETTE:	If that's all I was owed, I'm sure I'd have been paid off by now.
MERCADET:	Steady now. You should also know that I'm on the point of marrying off my daughter.
VIOLETTE:	I have two daughters. They slave away without the least hope of marrying because the earning capacity of honest women is very limited. Under the circumstances, of course, I wouldn't bother you but... my wife and daughters await my return in agony. At my age, there's so little I can do. Perhaps you could find me a place somewhere?
MERCADET:	Your name has been put down for the post of cashier in my new insurance company, which, all being well, should... Well, I won't bore you with the details.

HE PULLS OUT SOME MONEY.

VIOLETTE:	My wife and daughters will bless you! (ASIDE) The others who pester him get nothing. At least my approach has some effect.
MERCADET:	Here are sixty francs.
VIOLETTE:	In gold! It's a long time since I've seen that. At home they'll -
MERCADET:	There's just one thing -
VIOLETTE:	Don't worry, I won't say a word.
MERCADET:	It's not that. You must promise me not to come back for at least a month.
VIOLETTE:	A month! We can't live for a month on this!

MERCADET:	You really have nothing else?
VIOLETTE:	All I possess is what you owe me.
MERCADET:	(ASIDE) Poor man, he makes even me seem rich. (ALOUD) But I thought you had several little business loans out in the Quartier de l'Estrapade?
VIOLETTE:	Since they moved the debtors' prison, the business just isn't there.
MERCADET:	Couldn't you get some backing for that insurance company with the cashier's post I mentioned?
VIOLETTE:	I do have some friends who might consider -
MERCADET:	Well then, maybe they'd like to take out some shares.
VIOLETTE:	Alas, monsieur, no one wants to hear about shares any more. You speculators have lead everyone a merry dance just once too often.
MERCADET:	Oh well, farewell then. We'll settle as soon as we can. And you'll be the first to be paid.
VIOLETTE:	Thank you. And good luck with the marriage! My wife and daughters will say a prayer for Mademoiselle Mercadet.
MERCADET:	It would be much appreciated.

VIOLETTE GOES OUT.

MERCADET:	Ah, if only all my creditors were like him... On second thoughts, maybe not. He always manages to get money out of me.

VERDELIN ENTERS.

VERDELIN:	Good day, my friend. What is it you want from me?
MERCADET:	Your question gives me no chance to sugar the pill. You've seen through me already.
VERDELIN:	Listen, I haven't any money and, to be perfectly honest, if I did have, I wouldn't give it to you. I've already lent you as much as I can possibly afford. I've never asked for it back because I'm your friend as well as your creditor. And frankly, if I wasn't grateful for all you've done, the creditor would have killed off the friend long ago. Everything has its limits.
MERCADET:	Friendship perhaps but not misfortune.
VERDELIN:	If I was rich enough to wipe out all your debts, I'd do it without a moment's hesitation - I admire your courage. But, alas, you're bound to go under this time. Your recent enterprises have been brilliantly conceived as usual and plausible enough to take a number of people in - but they've still collapsed about your ears. You've fallen into disrepute. Nobody trusts you any more. You should have got out while the going was good. Of course, there'll always be bread for you at my house. But it's the duty of a friend to speak frankly.
MERCADET:	That way the friend can thoroughly enjoy himself. Not only can he demonstrate that he's wise and rich and his friend's poor and foolish but he can rub his friend's nose in the

	fact. So I'm thoroughly discredited, am I?
VERDELIN:	That's putting it too strongly. I'd say you're seen as an honest man forced to take risks which -
MERCADET:	Which haven't paid off. It's the lack of success people don't like not the means used. I'll prove it to you. This morning I've engineered a fall in the price of Lower Indre mine shares. Just so that you can make a killing buying them cheap - before that engineers' report you've paid a fortune to suppress is finally released and sends the prices sky high again.
VERDELIN:	You've really done it? (EMBRACING HIM) My good old friend, that's just like you!
MERCADET:	So now you understand - I don't need to be lectured and I don't need to be embraced, I just need money. And I'm not asking it for myself, it's for my daughter's marriage. We're completely broke. Behind the luxury, need lurks in every corner. Credit, promises, pleas - everything's used up. If I can't pay for certain essential expenses in cash then the marriage won't go ahead. So I need a fortnight of apparent prosperity - in the same way as you need another twenty-four hours of deceit on the Bourse. Verdelin, I won't ever ask you again. I've only one daughter. It's painful to admit this but my wife and Julie don't even have the necessary outfits - (ASIDE) He's hesitating.

VERDELIN:	(ASIDE) He's spun me so many yarns I don't know whether his daughter's getting married or not.
MERCADET:	This very day I have to give a dinner for my future son-in-law. A mutual friend is bringing him over. But I haven't even got my silverware - it's been... well, you know. So not only do I need three thousand francs, I also hope that you and your wife will join us - and lend us your dinner service.
VERDELIN:	Three thousand francs! Mercadet, no one has three thousand francs - to lend, that is. Most people barely have that much themselves - and if they lent it, well, they wouldn't have it any more, would they?
MERCADET:	(ASIDE) He's coming round. (ALOUD) You may choose not to believe me but honestly, nothing else matters once my daughter is married. My wife will be able to find a home with Julie. And, as for myself, I shall seek my fortune elsewhere. You're right, of course. I've said as much myself. I've made fortunes for others but when it comes to myself, nothing works out. I excel in the planning stages - the conception, the announcement, the prospectus, the organisation of the company - but when the time comes to reap the reward, I always miss out on the harvest.
VERDELIN:	Do you want to know why that is?
MERCADET:	Tell me.
VERDELIN:	It's because although you have imagination in abundance, you lack

	judgement. Imagination earns us admiration, judgement earns us money.
MERCADET:	(ASIDE) There's something in that. I never make a killing for myself. (ALOUD) Listen, Verdelin, I love my wife and daughter. Amidst my recent troubles, they have been my only consolation. They have been so gentle and patient! I want to see them protected from hardship. It's their plight that affects me most deeply - please, excuse my tears. You too have a charming little daughter. You wouldn't want to see her in the years to come dragged down by drudgery and unhappiness now would you? But that could be my devoted Julie's fate. Oh, my friend, I've drunk deep from the bitter chalice. I've created monopolies only to have them stolen from me. I've dreamed up schemes only to see them crumble to dust before my very eyes. But that is nothing, nothing, compared with the sadness of seeing myself deserted by you in my hour of greatest need. But perhaps it's better not to think about it. I don't want to trade on your pity.
VERDELIN:	Three thousand francs! But what do you want them for?
MERCADET:	(ASIDE) It's working. (ALOUD) My dear friend, a son-in-law is a timorous beast. The least whiff of poverty startles him away. The dresses for my wife and daughter are ordered. The suppliers are bringing them round. Yes, I've had the

impudence to say I'll pay for everything - relying on you. And then there's the dinner. We must have exquisite wines. On no account must the potential lover stay sober. We still have to keep up the pretence of wealth before Monsieur de la Brive at all times. Verdelin, a thousand écus won't kill you. You're getting sixty thousand francs in rents. And it's to save the life of a poor child you know you love. Julie plays so happily with your little girl - will you let your daughter's best friend perish in poverty?   As you sow so shall you -

VERDELIN: My friend, how many more times? I don't have three thousand francs. I can lend you my silver but as for the money -

MERCADET: How about a bank draft then? It's soon signed and -

VERDELIN: I'm sorry, I can't.

MERCADET: It's all over then. Oh my poor child! May God forgive me if I end this miserable dream that is my existence in the hope of waking in the security of His bosom.

VERDELIN: But haven't you found the son-in-law?

MERCADET: Oh yes, I've found one. Refuse me the means to make my daughter happy but don't insult me by calling me a liar. You shall see Monsieur de la Brive. I must have sunk low if you think I would... Oh, Verdelin, I wouldn't have believed this of you - not for three thousand francs. The

	only way for you to find forgiveness is to hand them over to me.
VERDELIN:	Very well. I'll go and see what I can do.
MERCADET:	That's just another way of saying no.
VERDELIN:	But what if the marriage falls through? Of course - why didn't I think of it before? When the marriage has taken place, I'll certainly give you the money.
MERCADET:	But the marriage won't take place without the three thousand francs!!! Is it possible that a man rolling in money like you, whom I've seen spend that sort of money on a passing fancy, won't give your friend a share?
VERDELIN:	(LAUGHING) Shares aren't looking too good at present.
MERCADET:	(LAUGHING TOO) Oh yes, very good. You're laughing now - that's something. After all, we've been through a lot together, haven't we, you and I? The things we got up to in the old days!
VERDELIN:	Remember that party at Rambouillet when I got into a fight with a guards officer on your behalf?
MERCADET:	Yes, but then I gave up Clarisse on your account. Ah, we were young then - and today we both have daughters to marry. If Clarisse were alive, she'd tell you off for refusing to help me.
VERDELIN:	If Clarisse were alive, I wouldn't be married!
MERCADET:	Ah yes, you were in love alright! So - I can count on you for dinner and

	you'll give me your word of honour to send me -
VERDELIN:	The dinner service -
MERCADET:	And the three thousand francs -
VERDELIN:	For the last time - I can't!
MERCADET:	Very well - so be it. I die, murdered by my best friend. You are insensible both to the memory of Clarisse and the despair of a father. There's nothing for it. I shall go and blow my brains out.

JULIE AND MADAME MERCADET ENTER.

MADAME:	Whatever's the matter?
JULIE:	Your voice scared me, father.
MADAME:	But Verdelin's with you. You can't be in danger.
JULIE:	Monsieur - has something happened between you and my father?
MERCADET:	You see, Verdelin? The sound of just a single anguished cry and they come running to me like two guardian angels. Tell me, Verdelin, do you really want to destroy a family like this? Their display of tender concern gives me the courage to fall on my knees before you.

JULIE STOPS HER FATHER FROM KNEELING.

JULIE:	No, father, let me plead on your behalf - if, as I suspect, it concerns money. Monsieur, I'm going to earn my own living so I can be the guarantor. Oblige my father just this

	once - please. He must be in great distress to beg like this.
MERCADET:	Dear child! (ASIDE) What heartfelt tones! I couldn't do it for real like that.
MADAME:	Monsieur Verdelin, render him this service. We'll be eternally grateful and I'll make use of all the means that are left me to -
VERDELIN:	You don't know what he's been asking for?
JULIE:	No.
VERDELIN:	Three thousand francs to marry you off.
JULIE:	Oh, monsieur, forget what I've just said to you. I don't wish for a marriage brought about by the humiliation of my father.
MERCADET:	(ASIDE) She's brilliant.
VERDELIN:	(SHAME-FACED) Listen, I'll - I'll go and get you the money.

HE GOES OUT.

JULIE:	Father, why didn't you tell me?
MERCADET:	(EMBRACING HER) You've saved us. And when I'm rich and powerful again, I'm going to make him pay for this.
JULIE:	But he's going to give you the money you asked for.
MERCADET:	Yes - but at too great a price. When I was in the position to give out favours, I did it with some grace. Not him - and he'll pay for it. Oh yes, Verdelin, you grudged lending me three thousand francs and so I won't have the least scruple about cheating you out of thirty thousand.

MADAME:	Don't be unfair. He did agree.
MERCADET:	Only because of Julie's pleading. He's had more than three thousand francs' worth of humiliation out of me.

VERDELIN COMES BACK, CARRYING A BAG OF MONEY, FOLLOWED BY JUSTIN WITH TWO MORE. JUSTIN THEN LEAVES.

VERDELIN:	It so happens I had the money in my carriage - for Brédif. But according to the porter, he's not in. So here it is - in three bags.
MERCADET:	Ah!
MADAME:	Monsieur, you can rely on a mother's gratitude.
VERDELIN:	In fact, it's solely to you and your daughter I'm lending this money, Madame. Perhaps you'd be good enough to both put your signatures on the promissory note Mercadet is going to give me.
JULIE:	Adding my signature - to ensure my own unhappiness!
MADAME:	(TO JULIE) Don't say anything just now.

MERCADET WRITES THE PROMISSORY NOTE.

MERCADET:	My dear Verdelin, at last I recognise in you the man I know and love. Should this include the interest?
VERDELIN:	No, no interest. I don't want to make a profit, just to help you.
MERCADET:	Julie, this is your second father.

JUSTIN RE-ENTERS FOLLOWED
BY VIRGINIE.

JUSTIN: Monsieur Minard is here.

JUSTIN LEAVES.

VIRGINIE: Madame, the tradesmen have brought everything.

MADAME: (SIGNING THE NOTE AND GIVING IT TO VERDELIN) I'm coming.

MERCADET: (TO VERDELIN) You see - just in time!

VERDELIN: In that case, I'll leave you.

MADAME MERCADET GOES
OUT WITH VIRGINIE.
VERDELIN IS SHOWN OUT BY
MERCADET WHO INDICATES
FOR MINARD TO COME IN.
AS HE ENTERS, JULIE COMES
UP TO HIM.

JULIE: If you wish to show the world that our love fears nothing, then be brave.

MINARD: What's happened?

JULIE: A man has presented himself as my husband. He's young and rich and my father has no pity for our plight.

MINARD: Don't worry, I shall convince him.

MERCADET: (RETURNING) So you love my daughter, monsieur?

MINARD: Yes, monsieur.

MERCADET: At least you've managed to convince my daughter you love her - which isn't quite the same thing.

61

MINARD:	If you weren't Julie's father, I would take offence at that suggestion. How could I not love Julie? Abandoned by my parents, knowing no other protection than that of the worthy Monsieur Duval, who's been as a father to me, I have only experienced the joys of true affection through knowing your daughter, Mademoiselle Julie is at once a sister and a friend. She is my whole family. She needed only to smile on me, to give me the slightest encouragement, to be loved beyond words.
JULIE:	Shall I stay, father?
MERCADET:	(ASIDE) You're enjoying this, aren't you? (TO MINARD) Monsieur, I have strict ideas on the subject of love between young people. You may think I'm being unduly sceptical but, unlike other fathers, I am not blind to the nature of my offspring. I see Julie as she really is. I wouldn't say that she is ugly but her beauty is unlikely to set the Seine in fire.
MINARD:	You're mistaken, monsieur. I dare to suggest you don't really know your own daughter.
MERCADET:	I know her perfectly well.
MINARD:	No, forgive me, you see Julie as everybody else sees her. Love transfigures her. When she is alone with me, her tenderness and devotion endow her with a very special sort of beauty.
JULIE:	Father, I'm embarrassed.

MERCADET:	I should think you're delighted if these are the sort of things he usually says.
MINARD:	I could say them a hundred, a thousand, times, and it still wouldn't be enough. It's not a crime to repeat them in front of her father.
MERCADET:	Well, up to now I've thought of myself as her father but you are the father of a Julie I'd very much like to meet. Come on, young man, open your eyes! The many beauties of her soul may, I allow, alter the expression of her countenance - but they don't do much for her complexion. There's no disguising the fact that her features are, well, a little unfortunate.
JULIE:	Father -
MINARD:	You have obviously never loved.
MERCADET:	On the contrary!
MINARD:	But that was in the past. Today we have a finer view of love.
MERCADET:	And what is that, pray?
MINARD:	We look towards the soul - towards the ideal.
MERCADET:	Ah, so that's what makes my daughter so beautiful! If a woman has a bad figure then the problem's solved by the ideal. The ideal also gives her lovely eyes and tiny feet - it tapers her stumpy fingers - while the soul is busy at work on her complexion.
MINARD:	Undoubtedly.
MERCADET:	Under the Empire, we used to call that -
MINARD:	Love! Holy and pure love!
MERCADET:	Love with the blindfold on.

JULIE:	Father, don't make fun of two children -
MERCADET:	You're not that young -
JULIE:	Who love each other with a passion true, pure and lasting. Who are confident that their mutual loved will see them safe through the vicissitudes of life. Two children who also love you deeply.
MINARD:	(TO MERCADET) She's an angel!
MERCADET:	(ASIDE) I'll give you angel! (TO JULIE) You've said enough, Julie. (TO MINARD) So, monsieur, you love Julie. She's charming, she's full of soul, of feeling, of heart. Indeed, if that's what you mean by beauty, then I suppose she fits the bill.
MINARD:	You do understand then!
MERCADET	And you love her without reservation?
MINARD:	I do.
JULIE:	What did I tell you, father?
MERCADET:	(TAKING THEM BY THE HANDS AND DRAWING THEM TO HIM :) Happy children! You're truly in love? What a glorious romance! (TO MINARD) And you really wish to marry her?
MINARD:	Yes, monsieur.
MERCADET:	Whatever the obstacles?
MINARD:	I've come here in order to overcome them.
MERCADET:	And nothing will discourage you?
MINARD:	Nothing.
JULIE:	Didn't I tell you that he loved me?
MERCADET:	Well, it seems you were right! Where could you hope to see a prettier sight than this? It does a

	father's heart good to see his daughter loved as she deserves.
JULIE:	Aren't you glad that I'm bringing you a son-in-law full of noble sentiments, blessed with a courageous soul, a -
MINARD:	Mademoiselle, please...
MINARD:	Oh yes, Adolphe, I can also speak out when I have to.
MERCADET:	Julie, go and see your mother. Monsieur Minard and I need to discuss rather more mundane matters. However elevated one's view of the female soul, there's still the matter of paying the rent.

JULIE LEAVES.

MERCADET:	Well, monsieur, now we're alone, we can talk frankly. You're not in love with my daughter.
MINARD:	Monsieur, I know you have a rich match in mind for Julie. Perhaps you think your daughter's inclinations don't matter. But you must understand that I wouldn't have come here and asked for her hand without first obtaining her heart.
MERCADET:	Yes, I think I've grasped the elevated nature of your love but things have reached the point where I need the whole truth. Have you written to each other?
MINARD:	Oh yes, letters filled with love.
MERCADET:	(ASIDE) She's been reading love letters, poor girl. No wonder her brain's gone soft! (ALOUD) Monsieur Minard, angels may possess a thousand perfections

	without having a single share in the bank. In Julie's case -
MINARD:	I'm prepared for any sacrifice. I only want Julie.
MERCADET:	And no obstacle will deter you, I think you said?
MINARD:	None.
MERCADET:	Well, then I'm going to confide in you a secret on which the honour and repose of the family you are so keen to join depends.
MINARD:	(ASIDE) What's he going to say?
MERCADET:	To be brutally frank, I am completely and utterly ruined, totally without financial resource. So, if you want Julie, she's yours. She'll be better off in your home, however poor, than here with us. Not only has she no dowry, she is burdened with parents who are poor - worse than poor in fact.
MINARD:	Worse than poor! That's not possible.
MERCADET:	I'm afraid it is. We are crippled with debt.
MINARD:	(ASIDE) He's playing a game with me. He wants to test me but I'm not falling for an old trick like this. (ALOUD) Well, monsieur, I'm young, I'm energetic and I'm ambitious - the world lies before me. As yet my name means nothing to anyone but I aim to succeed. I will have the joy of making the woman I love rich.
MERCADET:	I appreciate what you're saying. I've ruined myself trying to maintain my wife in the luxury to which she'd become accustomed. I too have sacrificed my life to an ideal but

66

	unfortunately creditors don't appreciate qualities like energy and imagination.
MINARD:	(ASIDE) This has to be a joke. He's rolling in it.
MERCADET:	So you're not worried by this little confidence of mine?
MINARD:	Not at all. No thought of personal gain soils my love.
MERCADET:	Well said, young man. That last phrase was particularly well turned, I felt. (ASIDE) He won't give up easily. (ALOUD) Let me be absolutely clear - you love my daughter so much that you'd pay any price for your happiness?
MINARD:	I would give my life for her.
MERCADET:	A love that noble deserves reward.
MINARD:	So then you -
MERCADET:	I trust you entirely.
MINARD:	You are right to.
MERCADET:	Wait here.

MERCADET LEAVES.

MINARD:	In my place, plenty of young men would have caved in. When a father that rich has a daughter who isn't that beautiful - and, after all, Julie's no more than passable - then I don't blame him to trying to find out if she's being married for her money. In fact, for a timid youth, I was magnificent. The father's no fool but there's no doubt Julie loves me. I'm the only one who's ever spoken words of love to her - and, well, one thing leads to another and I've sort of come to believe what I was telling

67

her. But I will make her happy. I love her as you ought to love your wife. Yes, damn it, I really do love her. If you take on the project of getting to know someone, then you end up knowing them properly - seeing the soul beneath the flesh as it were. And it's true what I told her father - she does have a beautiful soul. In fact, that's probably a sounder basis for a happy marriage than if she was a raving beauty. After all, there are plenty uglier. And if a woman loves you, she learns how to make herself seem pretty - doesn't she?

MERCADET ENTERS WITH FILES OF PAPERS.

MERCADET: Here, my dear son-in-law, are all the family papers which will show you exactly how rich we really are... No, no, please read. Here's the writ for the seizure of our furniture. The landlord wanted to sell off what was left and I've had to make a most disadvantageous deal to hold on to it. And here are a mass of orders for the seizure of this and that - writs for my arrest, that sort of thing. So you can see just how serious the situation is. Oh, and here are all my protests, my judgements and my dossiers all neatly classified. Always remember, young man, when your life is a mess, be sure to keep your papers in order. That way you maintain a measure of control while your life falls apart.

	What can a creditor say when he sees his debt properly numbered and filed? I've modelled myself on the government - everything in alphabetical order. Unfortunately, I've yet to begin even tackling the debts filed under 'A'.
MINARD:	You've paid nothing?
MERCADET:	Next to nothing. You can see I'm being frank with you.
MINARD:	Extremely.
MERCADET:	You understand book-keeping - look there. Debit total - three hundred and eight thousand francs.
MINARD:	(FAINTLY) Everything certainly seems to be in order.
MERCADET:	Thank you. I'm sorry about all this but I'm sure it's for the best. A father intent on getting rid of his daughter by fair means or foul would have tried to deceive you. He would have talked of some magnificent fictitious dowry to whet your appetite - it's often done. Plenty of fathers would simply exploit a love like yours. But you are dealing with an honourable man - broke but honourable. I was very worried on your behalf when you kept going on and one about your disinterested love in front of my daughter. It's a bold man who marries a penniless girl when he's only got a couple of thousand francs himself.
MINARD:	I - I think I'm about to make your daughter very unhappy.
MERCADET:	You mean that your eyes have finally registered the true state of her complexion?

MINARD:	Yes.
MERCADET:	Well, I admire you. You've lied with great aplomb. Maybe Julie's right. Maybe you would make a successful cabinet minister. But perhaps you don't agree?
MINARD:	Monsieur -
MERCADET:	Now it seems to me that I'm the injured party here. You've disturbed the peace of my family. You've filled my daughter's head with romantic notions which will make it very difficult for her to re-adjust to the real world. She's only a few months older than you and she was defenceless against your protestations.
MINARD:	But, monsieur - I know we can't marry now but don't blame me entirely. I do love your daughter. Where could a poor disinherited youth like me find a better wife?
MERCADET:	I've had quite enough of empty phrases. You must right the wrong you've done.
MINARD:	Believe me -
MERCADET:	Belief no longer comes into it. You must hand over to me all the letters my daughter wrote to you.
MINARD:	This very day.
MERCADET:	And you must also help an unhappy father to marry Julie off. It's essential to get her both a fortune and a name. You might even be useful. There's nothing dishonourable about playing the role of the rejected lover. Here in France, everyone wants what everyone else wants. It increases a girl's appeal if other men seem to be

	interested. And if our success plunges them into despair - then all the better. Envy lurks at the bottom of every human heart like the viper in his hole. You get my drift? ... As for my daughter - (HE CALLS JULIE) I'll leave you the unpleasant task of preparing her for the change in your intentions. If I told her, she simply won't believe me.
MINARD:	How can I - after all I've said and written?
MERCADET:	That, I'm afraid, is your problem.

MERCADET LEAVES.

MINARD:	I wish I was buried ten foot under! But how can I marry her? My salary isn't enough for one to live on, let alone two - or three if we have a baby. Here she comes. Somehow she doesn't seem the same. I suppose I'm used to seeing her with a dowry of three hundred thousand francs attached. (SIGHS) Here we go.

JULIE ENTERS.

JULIE:	Adolphe, what's happened?
MINARD:	Mademoiselle -
JULIE:	Mademoiselle? So I'm not Julie any more? Haven't you arranged everything with my father?
MINARD:	Well, yes - in a way...
JULIE:	Money has always been an enemy to love but I was sure you'd win him over.

MINARD:	Julie, your father has some powerful reasons... some very powerful reasons... and...
JULIE:	What exactly did he say? Adolphe, you don't seem to love me any more.
MINARD:	Of course, I still love you. It's just that...
JULIE:	My heart is turning to ice.
MINARD:	There's been a major change in our circumstances.
JULIE:	There are still obstacles?
MINARD:	Your father hadn't previously explained his situation fully. It's terrible for us, Julie, because it condemns us to unhappiness. Some men are energised by unhappiness, I know - but I'm not like that. It just depresses me - and I'd hate to see you unhappy too.
JULIE:	Then I'll have to have the courage for both of us. You'll always see me with a smile on my face - and I won't cost you anything. My painting should bring in as much as your salary. Without being rich, we can still be comfortable in our modest little household.
MINARD:	(ASIDE) Only girls without money love like this.
JULIE:	What did you say?
MINARD:	I said I never saw you so lovely. (ASIDE) She's being driven crazy by love. I must put an end to this. (ALOUD) Julie, this is all very well but -
JULIE:	But what? 'But' is a very insidious little word.
MINARD:	Your father appealed to my better nature. He showed me that love can

	sometimes be selfish. He convinced me of how important it is that you become rich. Julie, there are two kinds of love.
JULIE:	I thought there was only one.
MINARD:	No, a love which condemns you to miserable poverty is a selfish love. A love which sacrifices itself to make you happy is truly heroic.
JULIE:	My only happiness is to be with you.
MINARD:	Then you haven't heard your father on the subject. He insisted that I gave you up.
JULIE:	And have you given me up?
MINARD:	I'm trying to - but somehow I can't. (PAUSE) I know I must seem selfish and greedy but I'm trying to be honest. I'm alone in the world and we've no prospects. I thought you'd have enough to provide a basis for all the endeavours I dreamed of making on your behalf. Perhaps I even thought you'd be pleased that you'd helped me to succeed - that it'd make you love me still more. Even now, if my faith in myself were as strong as my love for you, I'd say - let's face the world together.
JULIE:	But you're not saying it.
MINARD:	I can't - although something tells me that I'll never be loved by anyone as I am by you.
JULIE:	Please don't talk about my love -
MINARD:	I know that in sacrificing that, I'm -
JULIE:	Go now, monsieur - please. Adieu.

MINARD LEAVES.

JULIE:	He's gone, never to return. Beauty, the only asset that can't be acquired, however illusory its nature, has let me down. I've tried to make up for it by tenderness, gentleness and obedience. I've been prepared to devote myself to the worship of the man I love - but my idol has feet of clay! The ugly girl's dream is over! I will never hope to give or receive happiness again. No more illusions, let's wake to reality. (SHE WIPES AWAY SOME TEARS) Look, I'm crying without even noticing my tears. I'll be alone now. He never loved me. I've invested a phantom with all my own qualities, all my own feelings - and now the phantom's fled! And my pain will seem so ridiculous to everyone else that I'd be wise to conceal it. Come, one last sigh over my lost love and then I'll resign myself to my fate - like so many other women.

MADAME MERCADET ENTERS.

MADAME:	Come along now, Julie. It's time to try on your dress. Monsieur de la Brive and Monsieur de Méricourt will be here shortly. You don't want them to catch you unprepared. (PAUSE) Monsieur Minard's gone then?
JULIE:	Oh yes.
MADAME:	Well, perhaps it's for the best. Your father really depends upon this marriage, you know.

JULIE:	Don't worry, mother. In order to save him I shall become Madame de la Brive.
MADAME:	It's the only hope he's got.

SHE LEADS HER DAUGHTER OUT.

END OF ACT ONE.

ACT TWO

ONE

AFTERNOON. JUSTIN SHOWS IN
DE LA BRIVE AND MERICOURT.

JUSTIN: The ladies are still getting dressed so they've asked if you'll be kind enough to wait a moment. Monsieur will join you shortly.

JUSTIN GOES OUT.

MERICOURT: Well, my friend, here you are - in Mercadet's lair. Soon you'll be officially betrothed to Mademoiselle Mercadet. But a word of caution - the father's a sly fox.

DE LA BRIVE: That's what scares me. He's bound to make difficulties.

MERICOURT: Not necessarily. Mercadet's a speculator. One day he's rich, the next day he's poor. From the little I've gleaned from the wife about his affairs, he'll probably be delighted to put a portion of his fortune in his daughter's name - and acquire a son-in-law who can give him a helping hand.

DE LA BRIVE: Chance would be a fine thing! But what if he wants to take up my references?

MERICOURT: I've given the wife excellent ones already. Smother any woman over forty with enough flattering attention

76

	and she'll believe everything you tell her.
DE LA BRIVE:	All the same...
MERICOURT:	You're not going to lose your nerve, are you? I know what a desperate situation you're in. If you weren't so close to despair, you wouldn't be contemplating marriage. For the true dandy marriage is a form of suicide. (SOTTOVOCE) Do you think you can last out?
DE LA BRIVE:	I'd be an outcast from smart society already if the beau monde didn't know me as de la Brive - and the bailiffs know me as Michonnin. Women have been the ruin of me. And nowadays rich Englishwomen with fat dowries going begging are like pugs - an extinct species.
MERICOURT:	You've tried gaming?
DE LA BRIVE:	Of course, but I prefer to leave it to the experts. I'm not stupid enough to risk my honour for a few trifling gains - usually followed by whacking great losses. It's getting harder all the time to get by. If you offer a moneylender a hundred thousand francs' worth of credit notes, he only gives you a measly ten thousand francs in cash. My tailor refuses to be impressed by my prospects. My horse exists on credit. And how my groom gets by, I really don't like to ask. All I have left to sell is my person. Oh, I know everyone will say terrible things about me. Look at him, a young man, highly regarded in the beau monde, not yet twenty-eight, a very

	presentable figure - and he's marrying the daughter of a rich speculator. The ugly daughter, I gather.
MERICOURT:	She's no beauty.
DE LA BRIVE:	You said it. But I don't see any alternative. Of course, the tried and tested way of making money is working. But I'm not cut out for that sort of thing. I may think I'm capable of doing anything - but deep down I know I'm not. A man like myself, formed for the finer flights of love, can hardly become a clerk or a civil servant. Society has failed to provide me with proper employment - and so I must do business with Mercadet. He's one of the biggest speculators in Paris and together we can conquer the commercial world. (PAUSE) You are quite certain he won't give his daughter less than one hundred and fifty thousand francs, aren't you?
MERICOURT:	You've seen Madame Mercadet at the Opera, haven't you? She's always so elegantly dressed, so -
DE LA BRIVE:	But I'm always elegantly dressed and I haven't got a sou.
MERICOURT:	Alright then, take a look around you. Everything here reeks of wealth. Can't you see how well-off they are?
DE LA BRIVE:	Yes, you're right. You can practically smell the money.
MERICOURT:	Besides, the mother has solid principles. In all the time I've known her, I've never caught the least whiff of anything that wasn't completely above board. So you will go through with it, won't you?

DE LA BRIVE:	Ready and willing. Yesterday at the club I managed to win enough to buy some suitable wedding presents. Well, enough for the deposit anyway. I'll settle the rest when I'm married.
MERICOURT:	So - apart from what you owe me - what exactly do your debts come to?
DE LA BRIVE:	Nothing very much really - a mere bagatelle! One hundred and fifty thousand francs - and I'm sure my father-in-law could renegotiate that down to fifty thousand. Then, with what's left over from the dowry, I shall launch into business. I've always said I'll only get rich when I've not a sou left to my name.
MERICOURT:	Mercadet's very sharp. He'll question you about your fortune. Are you prepared for that?
DE LA BRIVE:	Of course. I have the de la Brive estates, haven't I? Three hundred acres of land in Les Landes, which is worth thirty thousand francs - potentially forty-five thousand. If only we could start mining something or other on it then who knows how much it might be worth? That land's been a great asset to me.
MERICOURT:	And there's no turning back now?
DE LA BRIVE:	None. Particularly as I've decided on a political career.
MERICOURT:	You're wily enough.
DE LA BRIVE:	However, I shall start my career by becoming a journalist.
MERICOURT:	But you can't string two lines together.
DE LA BRIVE:	That's not necessarily a disadvantage. Some journalists write,

some don't. The ones who write are just the horses who pull the vehicle. The real power lies with the proprietors. They give the writers enough oats to live on and keep all the profits. I see myself as a proprietor - I've got the ideal cravat for it. I shall just sit there making pronouncements - "The question of the Orient is an important one for which it is not easy to find an answer" - "England, Messieurs, is never to be trusted." And if somebody is rambling on and you can't be bothered to listen, all you have to do is say in a loud voice, "We are marching into an abyss. The revolutionary process has not yet worked its way through." The key to being a successful proprietor, though, is never to say too much. You make remarks about articles in your paper that don't commit you too much one way or the other. Meanwhile you run about, you make yourself useful, you fix things for a minister he can't fix for himself. Finally, to complete the campaign, you publish a slim volume on some utopian proposal or other. It will be so well-written and so powerfully argued that nobody will ever open it though everybody will claim to have read it from cover to cover. Once you're got your reputation as a serious man, the rest is easy.

MERICOURT:　Too true, alas.

DE LA BRIVE:	The evidence is all around us. When you're finally invited to share in political power, they don't want to know what good you can do, they want to know what harm you can inflict. Talent is far less important than the ability to inspire fear. Everybody's very cautious in politics - because round each corner lurk piles of dirty linen that can never be washed clean. I've done my training in political theory already - I've wined, dined, gambled and got into debt. The day after my wedding, I shall be all prepared for a fresh start. I'll be grave. I'll be profound. I'll develop principles. Exactly <u>what</u> principles I haven't decided yet. The choice of principles on the menu here in France would put any restaurant owner to shame. I shall probably be a socialist. The word pleases me. In every epoch, my friend, there's always been the mot juste to unlock the door of ambition. Before 1789, one was an 'economist'. In 1805 everybody was a 'liberal'. Today the party heading for power calls itself 'socialist' - possibly because it's got absolutely nothing to do with socialism. In France a word always mean the opposite of what it's supposed to mean.
MERICOURT:	You've used your dissipation to good effect.
DE LA BRIVE:	I think I have.
MERICOURT:	But, between ourselves, don't you think you'll need a bit more than ballroom small talk? You'll need to

81

	know a bit about the subject, won't you?
DE LA BRIVE:	In commerce, in science, in the arts, you need special knowledge, talent, funds. But in politics you can get by on one phrase.
MERICOURT:	Which is?
DE LA BRIVE:	"The principles of my friends are my principles." You'll see.

MINARD ENTERS, CARRYING
THE LOVE LETTERS.

MINARD:	You are Monsieur de la Brive no doubt?
DE LA BRIVE:	I am indeed.
MERICOURT:	This is the youth the chambermaid told us about. He's been courting the heiress -
DE LA BRIVE:	To get the inheritance -
MERICOURT:	And now he's been turned down in favour of you.

DE LA BRIVE STUDIES MINARD
THROUGH HIS EYE-GLASS.

MINARD:	You are fortunate, monsieur. You have the privilege of wealth. When a young woman takes your fancy, you marry her.
DE LA BRIVE:	Monsieur, allow me to believe that, even without wealth, I might find it possible to succeed on my own merits.
MINARD:	Ah, if I had your wealth -
MERICOURT:	(ASIDE TO DE LA BRIVE) He wouldn't have much, poor boy -

MINARD:	I would not yield this treasure of grace and perfection to anyone. But you have also her father's approval.
DE LA BRIVE:	And you?
MINARD:	Alas, I have only my love for Mademoiselle Julie - a love whose loss I bitterly regret.

MERCADET ENTERS UNSEEN AND LISTENS.

DE LA BRIVE:	Monsieur, I'm not sure in what way I can assist you. (ASIDE TO MERICOURT) We may as well encourage the poor fellow a little. He may come in handy if the girl's impossibly ugly.
MINARD:	Monsieur, since chance has brought us together, I beg you from a grieving heart - make Mademoiselle Julie rich and happy.
MERCADET:	(ASIDE) Rich did he say? He'll spoil everything.

MERCADET COMES FORWARD.

MERCADET:	Ah, good day, Méricourt - have you seen my wife? (TO DE LA BRIVE) I'm sorry the women have kept you waiting - but you know how women are. (DRAWING MINARD ASIDE) Monsieur Minard, I thought we'd understood each other.
MINARD:	I was only doing as you asked.
MERCADET:	You seemed to be getting carried away. Not being quite as tactful as you might - if you get my drift.
MINARD:	Oh, I'm sorry. I hadn't realised.

83

DE LA BRIVE:	(TO MERCADET) He's no problem really.
MINARD:	(ASIDE TO MERCADET) I've brought Mademoiselle Julie's letters back.
MERCADET:	Go and hand them over to her mother then.
MINARD:	It nearly broke my heart re-reading them.
MERCADET:	Then perhaps you could manage a touch more sorrow as you depart. You don't look upset enough to have the desired effect. A big heart-felt sigh now - and then off you go.
MINARD:	I'm sorry, gentlemen, if I've disturbed you. But try and be understanding to a man who has lost all his happiness.
MERCADET:	(ASIDE TO MINARD) Bravo!

HE SHOWS MINARD OUT.

MERCADET:	Poor boy, he's besotted with my daughter. But you have to be cruel to be kind. He's only got ten thousand francs and a post as a book-keeper.
DE LA BRIVE:	He won't get far on that.
MERCADET:	Nowhere at all. Particularly as he was abandoned by his parents. Oh, he can be plausible. He worked out what Julie was worth and he managed to get my wife on his side. But he didn't get anywhere with me, I can assure you.
DE LA BRIVE:	You aren't the sort of man who gives away a jewel like your daughter to the first comer.
MERCADET:	Absolutely not. But, my dear monsieur, before the ladies arrive,

	we should perhaps spend a little time discussing serious matters.
DE LA BRIVE:	(TO MERICOURT) Here we go!
MERCADET:	Do you love my daughter?
DE LA BRIVE:	Passionately.
MERCADET:	(ASIDE) That doesn't bode well! (ALOUD) Passionately! Perhaps that's too grand an emotion for everyday use.
MERICOURT:	(ASIDE TO DE LA BRIVE) Don't overdo it. (ALOUD) My friend adores music and your daughter's voice sent him into ecstasy.
MERCADET:	Ah, he's heard her singing. Where exactly?
DE LA BRIVE:	At some banker's house... I can't recall the name...
MERCADET:	Verdelin?
DE LA BRIVE:	Verdelin! Yes, that's the name. Your daughter has so much soul.
MERCADET:	Ah, monsieur, I'm old-fashioned. I'm not a great one for the ideal. I go off to the Bourse and leave all that to my daughter who wanders about with her head full of poetry. She is, indeed, all soul. And you, I assume, are the same?
DE LA BRIVE:	No, not really.
MERCADET:	So how can you love Julie if you're not keen on the ideal?
MERICOURT:	(TO DE LA BRIVE) Think of something!
DE LA BRIVE:	I'm... full of ambition.
MERCADET:	That sounds more promising.
DE LA BRIVE:	Mademoiselle Julie is endowed with charming manners and a most distinguished bearing. She will be the ideal partner for me wherever my fortune as a politician leads me.

MERCADET:	Well, there's something in that. It's extremely rare for a minister or ambassador to find his perfect mate. You are a man of some sense.
DE LA BRIVE:	I'm also a socialist.
MERCADET:	Who isn't these days? But let us turn to business -
MERICOURT:	Can't we leave the details to the lawyers?
DE LA BRIVE:	Monsieur de Méricourt is right. That would suit us much better.
MERCADET:	All the same -
DE LA BRIVE:	Monsieur, my entire fortune rests in the de la Brive estate. It's been in my family for a hundred and fifty years and, God willing, it will never leave it.
MERCADET:	These days, of course, capital is preferable to land. If a revolution breaks out - and we've seen a few in our time, eh? - then we can take our capital with us wherever we want to go. Land meanwhile stays put like an idiot subject to all the taxes anyone sees fit to put on it. Still, it's not a serious obstacle. How much land do you have exactly?
DE LA BRIVE:	Three thousand acres, unentailed.
MERCADET:	Unentailed?
MERICOURT:	What did I tell you?
DE LA BRIVE:	Then there's the chateau -
MERCADET:	Go on.
DE LA BRIVE:	And, of course, there are the salt marshes nearby - which could give enormous yields if only the government gave permission for their exploitation.

MERCADET:	Monsieur, why haven't we met before? You mean, this land is by the sea?
DE LA BRIVE:	Half a league from it.
MERCADET:	And situated?
MERICOURT:	Near Bordeaux.
MERCADET:	Do you also have vineyards?
DE LA BRIVE:	No - but then it's difficult to get rid of the wine and vines cost such a lot to maintain. My land on the other hand hardly needs any maintaining at all. It was planted with pines by my grandfather, a far-sighted man who sacrificed himself for future generations. So you see, I possess -
MERCADET:	Just one moment. A businessman always likes to dot the i's and cross the t's.
DE LA BRIVE:	(TO MERICOURT) We're done for!
MERCADET:	You have your lands - and you have your salt marshes. I can see you could make a great deal from these marshes if properly advised. You might, for example, form a limited partnership to exploit the de la Brive salt marshes. You could raise more than a million that way without any problem.
DE LA BRIVE:	I am aware of that, monsieur. It's just a question of getting the right offer.
MERCADET:	(ASIDE) He's not a complete fool! (ALOUD) But what about your debts? Are the lands mortgaged? Because sometimes somebody can seem to own land which is, in fact, secretly controlled by his creditors.
MERICOURT:	Well, you wouldn't respect my friend here if he didn't have any debts now would you?

DE LA BRIVE:	I will be frank. The de la Brive lands have been mortgaged for forty five thousand francs.
MERCADET:	(ASIDE) That's nothing! (ALOUD) Young man, you have my consent. Consider it settled - you shall be my son-in-law.
DE LA BRIVE:	Thank you, monsieur.
MERCADET:	You really have no idea how lucky you are.
DE LA BRIVE: almost too well.	(TO MERICOURT) This is going
MERICOURT:	(TO DE LA BRIVE) He's spotted a chance for speculation and that's blinded him.
MERCADET:	(ASIDE) Of course, you need to get the government licenses - but grease the right palms and that's soon done. Then we start developing the salt-works. I'm saved! (ALOUD) Let me shake your hand English fashion. (HE SHAKES HIS HAND) We understand each other - you don't have the narrow outlook of the average provincial landowner.
DE LA BRIVE:	Monsieur, I hope you won't mind my asking for my part -
MERCADET:	What my daughter's fortune will be? Of course. She marries with everything she's entitled to. Her mother cedes to her - completely unentailed - her family property - a little farm of only two hundred acres but in excellent condition and situated right in the heart of Brie. I, for my part, will bestow on her two hundred thousand francs - though I feel it's best until you're properly settled to give you just the income

	from that - if that's agreeable. I want to be open with you, young man, because we're going to do business together. I like you and I like your style. You're ambitious then?
DE LA BRIVE:	Yes, monsieur.
MERCADET:	You like luxury and expense, you want to make a splash?
DE LA BRIVE:	Yes, monsieur.
MERCADET:	You want to play a leading role?
DE LA BRIVE:	Yes, monsieur.
MERCADET:	I guessed as much from your manner. I know mankind. You look like a man confident of a glittering future.
MERICOURT:	(ASIDE) In which he'll be permanently in debt.
MERCADET:	It suits me very well. I am past my prime. It's only right that somebody else should take the leading role in furthering our schemes.
DE LA BRIVE:	If I had to choose out of all the father-in-laws in Paris, I'd choose you. You're exactly what I have been looking for.
MERCADET:	Youth should enjoy itself. You and my daughter will take your place in society. You'll have a large apartment, carriages, servants, you'll give parties. Julie is a very lively girl and she'll fit in with all this perfectly. Just see that you're not one of those people who start with a bang and then fizzle away like a spent firework. Don't fritter your wife's fortune.
DE LA BRIVE:	Because if one doesn't succeed -

MERCADET:	Or if things start to get out of control -
DE LA BRIVE:	Then at least one has enough left for bread.
MERCADET:	Yes - but these days man does not live by bread alone. He has horses in the stable, a magnificent house. He has a box at the opera and he gives lavish dinner parties where the guests get a great deal more than bread.
DE LA BRIVE:	Let me shake your hand again English fashion, monsieur. You understand life.
MERICOURT:	(ASIDE) This is going suspiciously well.
DE LA BRIVE:	(ASIDE) He's fallen headfirst into my salt marshes.
MERCADET:	(ASIDE) He didn't insist on cash down - he's prepared to accept just the income.
MERICOURT:	(TO DE LA BRIVE) Are you satisfied then?
DE LA BRIVE:	Not quite. There is still the matter of my debts.
MERICOURT:	(TO DE LA BRIVE) Just a moment - (TO MERCADET) My friend is reluctant to tell you this but he's also too honest to try and hide that he does have a few debts here and there.
MERCADET:	Oh, don't worry - I understand these things perfectly. What's the damage then - the odd fifty thousand francs?
MERICOURT:	More or less.
DE LA BRIVE:	Yes... More or less.
MERCADET:	Let's leave them until you are married. It'll be a pleasure for your wife to be able to settle them for you. And, of course, they will be paid.

	(ASIDE) Out of the proceeds of the de la Brive salt-works. (ALOUD) It's a mere trifle. (ASIDE) All I have to do is value the salt yield a hundred thousand francs higher. I'm saved.
DE LA BRIVE:	(ASIDE) I'm saved.

MADAME MERCADET AND JULIE ENTER.

MERCADET:	Ah, here come my wife and daughter.
MERICOURT:	Madame, allow me to present to you my friend, Monsieur de la Brive, who admires your daughter -
DE LA BRIVE:	Passionately.
MERCADET:	(TO DE LA BRIVE) You like them dark, I gather. My daughter's complexion is, as you see, positively Spanish and therefore proof against the buffeting of age.
DE LA BRIVE:	I'd have hated her to be blonde.
MERCADET:	You'll see my daughter is absolutely right for a budding politician.

DE LA BRIVE STUDIES HER WITH HIS EYE-GLASS.

DE LA BRIVE:	Indeed, and most elegantly turned out. But then - like mother, like daughter. Madame, I place my hopes under your protection.
MADAME:	Since you are presented by Monsieur de Méricourt, monsieur, you are more than welcome.
JULIE:	(ASIDE) What an ass!
MERCADET:	(TO JULIE) He's extremely rich. We're all going to be millionaires.

	Come on now, you must be friendly - he's very charming.
JULIE:	What do you want me to say to him? It's the first time I've set eyes on him and you've already decided he's going to be my husband.
DE LA BRIVE:	Will mademoiselle allow me to hope she will not contradict my wish to make her mine?
JULIE:	My duty is to obey my father.
DE LA BRIVE:	(ASIDE) Proud as only an ugly woman can be. She'll expect more effort from me than a duchess would.
JULIE:	(ASIDE) He's rich, he's good-looking, so why is he wooing me? There's something odd here.
DE LA BRIVE:	(ASIDE) To battle! (ALOUD) Mademoiselle, you may well be unaware of the sentiments you have inspired in me. For two months I have been hoping that I might come and pay my respects.
JULIE:	I'm flattered by your attention, monsieur.
MADAME:	(TO JULIE) He's perfect.
JULIE:	Mother, let me find out for myself if I could really be happily married to this man.
MERCADET:	(TO MERICOURT) You can count on our gratitude, monsieur. We owe your our happiness - for if our daughter is happy then so are we.
MADAME:	I trust the gentlemen will do us the honour of staying for dinner. It's just an informal little affair.
MERCADET:	Yes, I hope you don't mind taking pot luck.
MADAME:	Perhaps you'll accompany us, Monsieur de Méricourt. (TO JULIE)

	We'll leave you to have a talk with him.
JULIE:	Thank you, mother.
MADAME:	Monsieur Mercadet?
MERCADET:	(TO DE LA BRIVE) She's romantic like all young people. I recommend taking the route of poetry.
DE LA BRIVE:	(TO MERCADET) Trust me. I am fully fluent in romanticism - it is the grammar of modern sentiment. Put simply, it is the art of making words speak louder than actions.
MERCADET:	(AS HE LEAVES) He's really too much, this young man!

JULIE AND DE LA BRIVE ARE LEFT ALONE.

JULIE:	You mustn't think it strange, monsieur, if I ask for some proof of your affection. When you're as plain as I am, you're bound to be a little sceptical.
DE LA BRIVE:	Your modesty only adds to your attraction, mademoiselle.
JULIE:	If I had the sort of beauty that turns heads, I'd find your pursuit of me perfectly comprehensible. But in order to love me, I feel you have to get to know me - and we are meeting for the first time.
DE LA BRIVE:	But there are inexplicable attractions which somehow -
JULIE:	You mean you love me without knowing why?
DE LA BRIVE:	The day you can fully explain what love is is the day it will cease to exist. It is the most beautiful of feelings simply because it creeps

	unannounced into our souls. The very first time I saw you -
JULIE:	So you've seen me before?
DE LA BRIVE:	Of course. I've loved you for six months. Ever since I heard you sing at that last concert at Monsieur Verdelin's. Your voice revealed to me the beauty of your soul.
JULIE:	What did I sing? Can you remember?
DE LA BRIVE:	(ASIDE) Damn it! (ALOUD) I can only recall the impression - which was delicious.
JULIE:	So you truly love me then?
DE LA BRIVE:	Mademoiselle, you are full of courage, of fine feelings, of ideas. You would know how to be a fitting companion for a rising politician - and how to create a salon here in Paris. Some men have made the mistake of lumbering themselves with unsuitable brides at the start of their careers. And, on the political ocean, if a woman is not a powerful tug-boat, she is simply a dead weight dragging her husband down to the bottom. I had never thought I would find someone who would be both sympathetic and an asset to my career. But I saw you and I said to myself - "With her by my side, I could be an ambassador!"
JULIE:	(ASIDE) Everybody's so ambitious these days! (ALOUD) So you're not only in love, you're also ambitious. There's calculation mixed in with the sentiment.

DE LA BRIVE:	(ASIDE) She's not stupid. (ALOUD) Mademoiselle, so many different elements go to make up love -
JULIE:	And in your love, complete devotion is, of course, included?
DE LA BRIVE:	Above all else.
JULIE:	So my family -
DE LA BRIVE:	Will become mine.
JULIE:	And nothing will stop you?
DE LA BRIVE:	Nothing.
JULIE:	You do know I'm in love with someone else?
DE LA BRIVE:	I met him just now. I have to admit it did worry slightly about your judgement. He's hardly worthy of you.
JULIE:	There you're wrong. I've only given him up because of my devotion to my father. If you save him from ruin then I will love you. I will completely forget a love I thought could never die - and I will become the most devoted, the most loving of wives and... (ASIDE) I think I'm going to faint!
DE LA BRIVE:	(ASIDE) 'Ruin' did she say? I don't like the sound of that. But maybe it's a test. It seems I have to go through a whole series of trials in order to be allowed to marry her - it's a bit like joining the Freemasons. (ALOUD) Mademoiselle, I hope to earn by my love all the devotion I for my part unconditionally offer to you. But please, stop putting my sincerity to the test. Your father and I are in complete agreement over all the financial arrangements.
JULIE:	Then he has told you everything?

DE LA BRIVE:	Everything.
JULIE:	So you do know he's ruined?
DE LA BRIVE:	Ruined! (ASIDE) That word again!
JULIE:	(ASIDE) Ah, I'm saved! (ALOUD) My father owes over three hundred thousand francs.
DE LA BRIVE:	He... owes... three... hundred...
JULIE:	Has something happened to your unquestioning devotion?
DE LA BRIVE:	(ASIDE) It'll take more than devotion for me to marry - If she thinks a rare being like myself hands himself over for the rest of his days for - for nothing....
JULIE:	Am I not the prize you sought then?
DE LA BRIVE:	(ASIDE) But Méricourt incapable of deceiving me like this...
JULIE:	So you don't love me after all?
DE LA BRIVE:	(ASIDE) Now I think about it, it has to be a trap. (ALOUD) Mademoiselle, even if your father owed millions, I would still marry you - because you are the woman I love. You played that little scene very well but I won't take back what I said - you will be a delightful ambassador's wife.

JUSTIN SHOWS IN PIERQUIN.

JUSTIN:	Mademoiselle, Monsieur Pierquin wishes to talk to your father - (SOTTOVOCE) I believe it's on the subject of Monsieur de la Brive.
JULIE:	(INDICATING) My father's through there.

JUSTIN GOES OUT.

PIERQUIN:	Mademoiselle, your humble servant.
DE LA BRIVE:	Pierquin here!

HE MOVES AWAY AND OSTENTATIOUSLY STUDIES THE PICTURES ON THE WALL WITH HIS EYE-GLASS.

PIERQUIN: (ASIDE) But that's my Michonnin over there! All is lost! Just when I've hurried over to get his letters of credit back from Mercadet because I'd heard on the grapevine the boy is finally marrying an heiress! That Mercadet has all the luck - he's managed to get him here in no time at all.

JULIE: Do you know Monsieur?

PIERQUIN: Oh yes, you little slyboots - and I expect you're in on the plot to make sure he stays here till he's done a deal. (ASIDE) Oh, I ought to have had a pretty niece.

JULIE: Who exactly is he then?

PIERQUIN: Why, he's Michonnin - a hopeless debtor. You make sure he stays here - and I'll go and fetch an officer.

JULIE: For Monsieur de la Brive?

PIERQUIN: He's known to us as Michonnin.

JULIE: Then he's not rich?

PIERQUIN: Him? He hasn't got two sous to rub together.

JULIE STARTS TO LAUGH.

PIERQUIN: (ASIDE) Mercadet's pulled a fast one! (ALOUD) Now listen - you keep him occupied. When I come back with the officer, we can deal with this fellow and your father can hand over the forty-seven thousand Michonnin owes me. There's no point in sending this one to prison - some pretty woman's bound to set him free.

JUSTIN RETURNS.

JULIE: (ASIDE) Imprisoned as well as married! It's too much for one man to cope with.

JUSTIN: (TO PIERQUIN) Monsieur, as you know, is occupied with the arrangements for mademoiselle's marriage and asks you to excuse him.

PIERQUIN: Her marriage to whom?

JUSTIN: (INDICATING DE LA BRIVE) Why, to the gentleman over there.

PIERQUIN: To him! You mean...? (ASIDE) Oh really, it's too much. One bankrupt marrying the daughter of another bankrupt! How they'll laugh on the Bourse. I must run over there and tell everyone the news.

HE LEAVES.
JUSTIN WITHDRAWS. JULIE AND DE LA BRIVE REMAIN.

JULIE: So you're really called Michonnin?

DE LA BRIVE: Yes, mademoiselle. It's our old family name. But like a lot of other people we changed our name ten years ago - to de la Brive. If you put Monsieur in front of it, it sounds much nicer. La Brive is actually a

	charming little farm bought by my late grandfather.
JULIE:	And that man was telling the truth - you are in debt?
DE LA BRIVE:	Oh yes, but trifles, nothing serious. I've told your father all about them.
JULIE:	So, monsieur, you're marrying me purely for love? (ASIDE) Let's at least get some amusement out of this. (ALOUD) I don't suppose my dowry came into it by any chance?
DE LA BRIVE:	Mademoiselle, you will find in me the most loving, the most loveable of husbands. As a socialist, completely dedicated to my political career, I will leave you the absolute mistress of your own fortune.
JULIE:	Except, of course, that I don't have a fortune.

MERCADET COMES IN AND OVERHEARS THIS.

MERCADET:	Julie, your passion for young Minard is leading you astray. It's making you slander your father -
JULIE:	Only in order to explain to Monsieur Michonnin here, who's crippled with debt himself, why he can't possibly marry a girl without a sou to her name.
MERCADET:	His name's Michonnin?
JULIE:	Michonnin de la Brive.
MERCADET:	Julie - leave us.
JULIE:	(SOFTLY TO HER FATHER) Pierquin's gone to get him arrested. I hope you'll stop him but I didn't know what to do.

MERCADET:	(CONSULTING HIS WATCH) The sun has gone down. Pierquin saw monsieur?
JULIE:	Yes.
MERCADET:	Then the game is lost.

JULIE GOES OUT.

DE LA BRIVE:	(ASIDE) If the wedding's still on, I won't just be a socialist, I'll become a communist.
MERCADET:	(ASIDE) Swindled by Méricourt, my wife's friend, just as if we were on the Bourse. It's enough to make you stop believing in God.
DE LA BRIVE:	(ASIDE) Courage now.
MERCADET:	(ASIDE) He's played me a dirty trick. I can afford to take the high ground. (ALOUD) Monsieur Michonnin, as I believe you're called, your conduct is despicable.
DE LA BRIVE:	In what way? Didn't I tell you I had debts?
MERCADET:	Indeed, debts are understandable. But where exactly is this land of yours?
DE LA BRIVE:	In Les Landes.
MERCADET:	And it consists of -
DE LA BRIVE:	Sands planted with firs -
MERCADET:	Suitable, no doubt, for the manufacture of toothpicks?
DE LA BRIVE:	Something along those lines.
MERCADET:	And it's worth?
DE LA BRIVE:	Thirty thousand francs.
MERCADET:	And it's mortgaged for -
DE LA BRIVE:	Forty-five thousand francs.
MERCADET:	You managed to bring that off?
DE LA BRIVE:	Oh yes.

MERCADET:	I'm impressed! And these salt-marshes -
DE LA BRIVE:	They're really very close to the sea.
MERCADET:	Close enough to be actually covered by the sea?
DE LA BRIVE:	The locals were mean enough to say so - and all my loans were stopped in their tracks.
MERCADET:	It's extremely difficult to float the sea - in shares, I mean.
DE LA BRIVE:	It's not even drinking water.
MERCADET:	It's certainly hard to swallow if that's what you mean. Monsieur, strictly between ourselves, your behaviour seems to me completely irresponsible.
DE LA BRIVE:	Oh, agreed! If only all this were just between ourselves.
MERCADET:	You transferred all your possessions to the name of a friend - I've seen a note of it among your files - and then you called yourself de la Brive but signed all your promissory notes Michonnin.
DE LA BRIVE:	Exactly - what then?
MERCADET:	What then? I'll make you suffer for this!
DE LA BRIVE:	Don't forget - I'm a guest in your house.
MERCADET:	With the help of this deception, you've attempted to enter a respectable household and abuse the trust of a devoted mother and father. You have pretended to be in love with my daughter. You have - (ASIDE) You know, it might be possible to make use of this young man now I come to think of it. He's got style, he's elegant, and he's

	bright. (ALOUD) In short, monsieur, you are -
DE LA BRIVE:	Not another word if you value your life!
MERCADET:	Are you threatening me now - your host?
DE LA BRIVE:	Just tell me - does your daughter have a dowry?
MERCADET:	Monsieur?
DE LA BRIVE:	(ASIDE) I've got him now. (ALOUD) Do you or do you not have the two hundred thousand francs?
MERCADET:	My daughter, monsieur, is a treasure beyond -
DE LA BRIVE:	So you don't have the money? But you're still asking me to venture my precious freedom? Isn't my person a valuable asset? Would you swindle your own son-in-law?
MERCADET:	These are strong words, monsieur.
DE LA BRIVE:	They are totally deserved.
MERCADET:	(ASIDE) you have to hand it to him - he's got guts.
DE LA BRIVE:	As I see it, I am the injured party. You took advantage of my inexperience.
MERCADET:	Inexperience! This from a man who can borrow against acres of sand for sixty per cent more than they're worth!
DE LA BRIVE:	Sand is used in making glass.
MERCADET:	So I've heard.
DE LA BRIVE:	Let's face it, monsieur, we share the same morality. Between ourselves -
MERCADET:	(ASIDE) I'm going to flatten him. (ALOUD) I think you're wrong there. You are my debtor and I will hold you to your debt. I have in your

	name forty-eight thousand francs in credit notes, interest and expenses - all given to me by Pierquin. I could have you put away for five years.
DE LA BRIVE:	Then I'll be your guest in prison too, that's all.
MERCADET:	So you take that tone, do you? You make a joke of your debts - of your signature?
DE LA BRIVE:	What do you make of them then?
MERCADET:	(ASIDE) Here's my chance! (ALOUD) Truthfully now, what is your situation?
DE LA BRIVE:	Desperate. Méricourt arranged to marry me off because I owe him thirty thousand francs on top of everything else.
MERCADET:	I see. I'm not going to waste time giving you moral advice. I assume you'd rather make some money -
DE LA BRIVE:	I wish you were my father-in-law!
MERCADET:	Alas, nothing plus nothing would still equal nothing. But I do have a notion. Listen to me -

ENTER MADAME.

MADAME:	Is monsieur still dining here?
MERCADET:	Of course. In desperate times food brings inspiration. (ASIDE) Besides, I need to question him further.
DE LA BRIVE:	I have an appetite born of despair.
MERCADET:	Then let's go and dine.
MADAME:	I hear Verdelin's carriage.
MERCADET:	Verdelin! What am I going to say to him?

VERDELIN IS SHOWN IN BY
JUSTIN, NOW IN A SMART
UNIFORM.

JUSTIN: Monsieur Verdelin -

VERDELIN: (TO MERCADET) I've not brought my wife and I don't expect to be staying myself.

MERCADET: He's furious! (TO DE LA BRIVE) Monsieur, if you would be good enough to accompany Madame? (TO MADAME) Leave us, my dear.

MADAME MERCADET, DE LA
BRIVE AND JUSTIN LEAVE.

MERCADET: Whatever is the matter?

VERDELIN: Is that your son-in-law?

MERCADET: Yes - and no.

VERDELIN: This is supposed to be your wonderful marriage?

MERCADET: (ASIDE) He knows everything. (ALOUD) The marriage, my dear Verdelin, will not be taking place. I was duped by Méricourt, whom I trusted. But surely -

VERDELIN: No ifs and buts. This morning you enacted one of your famous dramas - also featuring your wife and daughter - simply in order to extract three thousand francs from me. I should have known -

MERCADET: Don't finish - please. This is how people are judged when they're going through hard times. Everything they do is suspect. Why did I borrow your dinner service then? Why am I giving dinner? Would I have dressed my wife and daughter so

104

	magnificently if everything was hopeless? In any case, who told you the marriage was off?
VERDELIN:	Pierquin. I met him -
MERCADET:	Then word is out?
VERDELIN:	Everybody's laughing about the affair. Particularly about the pile of dud credit notes you got from your son-in-law. Pierquin told me that your creditors are all meeting up this evening at Goulard's so that they can all act in unison tomorrow.
MERCADET:	This evening! Tomorrow! The bell of bankruptcy has already started to toll!
VERDELIN:	There's also a move afoot to get all business speculators cleared from the floor of the Bourse.
MERCADET:	Idiots! And tomorrow they'll carry me away -
VERDELIN:	Off to the debtors' prison in a cab -
MERCADET:	The speculator's hearse! Still - let's go and dine.
VERDELIN:	No, thank you. The dinner would give me indigestion. It's cost me too much already.
MERCADET:	Verdelin, come and dine - without fear. Because tomorrow the Bourse will be forced to acknowledge that Auguste Mercadet is one of its masters. Oh yes, all my debts will be paid - and the house of Mercadet will be worth millions. Believe me - I will be the Napoleon of business - but this time, without the Waterloo!
VERDELIN:	And how about the troops?
MERCADET:	They - they will be paid. You'll see.

VERDELIN: Well, in that case, I'm delighted to dine. Long live Mercadet then - the Emperor of Speculators.

MERCADET USHERS VERDELIN IN THEN TURNS BACK.

MERCADET: He's believed me! There's time for one more try - for one last desperate throw of the dice! Tomorrow I'll be rolling in money again - or else I'll be fast asleep - wrapped in the watery blankets of the Seine.

HE GOES OUT.

TWO

NEXT MORNING. MERCADET ENTERS.

MERCADET: I've scarcely slept a wink. After I'd done what I had to do, I dozed off in a chair and had the most appalling nightmares. Bailiffs pursued me down dark streets. Dud shares poured down from the sky like huge snowflakes which threatened to bury me - while creditor-like vultures hovered expectantly. (HE SHUDDERS) Daylight was almost a relief. (PAUSE) But it does mean I can't put it off any longer. I have to find out how my moves have been received. It's now or never.

HE RINGS. JUSTIN ENTERS.

JUSTIN: Monsieur?
MERCADET: Good morning, Justin. Now you do understand, don't you, that Monsieur Godeau's arrival is to be kept secret?
JUSTIN: I'm afraid that's impossible, monsieur. Monsieur Brédif's already out and about. You see, when the coach arrived at two o'clock in the morning, it made such a noise that it woke everyone - including Monsieur Brédif. He thought at first you were fleeing for Brussels.
MERCADET: I pay good money to make sure -
JUSTIN: Monsieur is put out?
MERCADET: Oh well, it can't be helped, I suppose.

JUSTIN:	The coach was caked in mud but Pere Grumeau did notice that there wasn't any luggage on board.
MERCADET:	That's because Godeau was in such a hurry to be reconciled with me that he left his luggage behind in Le Havre to follow on. He's brought a rich cargo back from Calcutta, apparently, though his wife's still in the Indies. Oh yes, he's made an honest woman of her, you'll be pleased to hear. After she did leave everything, including her son, to go with him.
JUSTIN:	It was very lucky that Monsieur stayed up all night working. It meant that he -
MERCADET:	Was here to receive Godeau! Deputise for you, you mean - while you were carousing with all the rest. I expect you got very merry - eh, Justin?
JUSTIN:	We only drank what was left over.
MERCADET:	Now, I want you to listen carefully. Do your best to convince everyone that Godeau hasn't arrived. That will get my creditors off my back and I can settle with them on reasonable terms. Once they think he's here, they'll be like bees round the honeypot and I won't have a moment's peace. Oh - and send Pere Grumeau to fetch my broker -
JUSTIN:	Monsieur Berchut - rue des Filles-Saint-Thomas. I assume that Pere Grumeau can tell _him_ about Godeau's arrival?

MERCADET:	Justin, you'll go far! Off you go now - and make sure no one disturbs me until I call.

JUSTIN LEAVES.

MERCADET:	If I can make them all believe in Godeau's return then I'll gain eight days - and eight days is as good as a fortnight when it comes to settling bills. Now, in the name of Godeau, I'm going to buy three hundred thousand francs' worth of Lower Indre mine shares - and I'm going to do it early before Verdelin gets to the Bourse. When Verdelin does turn up, he'll still be thinking I'm hors de combat - not that he's bothered to confide in me about what he's up to - so my sly friend will start buying Lower Indre shares and in so doing, he'll set off the very rise in prices he's trying to avoid. And that's not all I've planned. Last night I wrote a letter using the name of some of the other shareholders to demand the publication of the favourable engineers' report Verdelin's money has been holding back. Berchut will make sure the letter appears in all the papers. In no time at all, Lower Indre shares will leap from just twenty five per cent to well above their face value. That leap should net me six hundred thousand. With three hundred thousand of that, I pay for the shares I've bought. With the other three hundred thousand, I pay off my creditors. I should be able to use the

name of Godeau to negotiate a discount of forty thousand or so on what I owe. Then I shall be free. I shall once again be king of the walk. (PAUSE) It's taken a lot of nerve though. I can't say it was easy going and ordering a coach from that place in the Champs Elysees at the dead of night -as if I was planning a moonlit flit. Then the coachman nearly ruined everything when we got back by blabbing out his thanks to me at the top of his voice. That'll teach me to over-tip. Still, so far, so good -

HE GOES TO THE BEDROOM DOOR.

Michonnin, the bailiffs are here.

A STARTLED DE LA BRIVE RUSHES IN.

MERCADET: Don't panic. That was just to wake you up.

DE LA BRIVE: A good drinking bout does for my brain what a downpour does for the countryside. It makes ideas bud forth, turn green and burst into flower. In vino varietas!

MERCADET: My dear friend, yesterday we were unfortunately interrupted right in the middle of a very interesting conversation.

DE LA BRVE: I remember it very well, father-in-law. We realised that our respective establishments were on the rocks. We were, as it were, heading for the tumbrel. You are unlucky enough to

110

	my creditor and I am honoured to be your humble debtor to the tune of forty seven thousand two hundred and thirty francs - plus the odd centime...
MERCADET:	So you've still got a clear head after last night.
DE LA BRIVE:	My head is as unencumbered as my pockets and my conscience. After all, why should anyone reproach me? I've given enormous benefit to the tradespeople of Paris, whether known personally to me or not. People like me idle? - Useless? We ensure the circulation of money.
MERCADET:	By circulating money, you mean?
DE LA BRIVE:	Exactly - and when I'd no more money left, I borrowed it at the most exorbitant rates. If money is regarded as a god nowadays, nobody can say that I've stopped short of idolatry.
MERCADET:	You have your wits about you.
DE LA BRIVE:	Alas, that's all I have about me.
MERCADET:	But it's your wits that we need just now. I will be brief -
DE LA BRIVE:	Do you mind if I sit down for this? You appear - as we gentlemen riders say - to have the bit between your teeth.
MERCADET:	Now, in business, there's nothing wrong with being smart. And being excessively smart is not the same as being unscrupulous - and unscrupulousness is not the same as roguery - and roguery is not the same as downright dishonesty.
DE LA BRIVE:	(ASIDE) He's not got me drunk because he likes me.

MERCADET:	Of course, these distinctions are subtle ones - and, of course, one must always stay just within the bounds of the Code Napoleon.
DE LA BRIVE:	Of course.
MERCADET:	If I may say so, you're already on the slippery slope that leads down the route I have already indicated. You've tasted full of the intoxicating fruits of Parisian life. Worldly pleasures have you in their toils. Your life is inconceivable without luxury. For you, Paris starts at l'Etoile and ends at the Jockey Club. It's filled with women about whose conquest you either boast noisily or keep very quiet indeed.
DE LA BRIVE:	Ah yes, indeed!
MERCADET:	It's the heady atmosphere of the corridors of power, of the theatre, of journalism. And either you must continue this existence - or else blow your brains out.
DE LA BRIVE:	I'm not sure I'd go quite that far!
MERCADET:	Then do you consider you have enough native wit left to maintain yourself in glossy boots and expensive vices? Do you have enough talent to stop your frail bark foundering on the rocks of the debtors' prison? Do you still believe there's some way out?
DE LA BRIVE:	You must be reading my mind. What do you want of me?
MERCADET:	I want to save you - by plunging you head first into the world of business.
DE LA BRIVE:	How do you propose to do that?

MERCADET:	Tell me - are you prepared to compromise yourself for me by pretending to be -
DE LA BRIVE:	In my experience, men of straw often burn.
MERCADET:	Not in this case. Help me out of my desperate plight and I will guarantee to give you your forty seven thousand two hundred and thirty francs - not forgetting those odd centimes. All that's needed of you is dexterity.
DE LA BRIVE:	With the pistol or with the sword?
MERCADET:	Nobody's going to be killed.
DE LA BRIVE:	That's a relief.
MERCADET:	On the contrary... I need to bring a man back to life.
DE LA BRIVE:	I'm sorry but that I cannot do. That sort of caper may go down very well in old farces but it's not so well received in real life. Particularly where the police are concerned.
MERCADET:	Then do I assume you'd prefer five years in the debtors' prison?
DE LA BRIVE:	Well... it depends what you want this revived person to do, of course. Provided my honour's intact and it's worth my while...
MERCADET:	All being well, your honour's not at risk and as for it being worth your while - well, we simply can't afford not to milk my idea for all it's worth. I have managed to hold on to my right to initiate businesses and set up companies. They've tried to cut down on the activities of speculators like myself but they've not got a hope of succeeding while there are shareholders greedy for quick

returns. If a business promises immediate gain on investment then nothing can stop it coming into being. The future can always be put up for sale - even if the odds are worse than the lottery. But there are plans to take away my seat at the table in the Bourse where these tasty speculative dishes are served. Help me keep my place and we'll gorge ourselves on the banquet! My friend, perhaps you hesitate. It's true that those who go looking for millions may have great difficulty in finding them - but those who never look find nothing at all.

DE LA BRIVE: (ASIDE) He's got a point there!

MERCADET: Well?

DE LA BRIVE: You'll release me from my debt?

MERCADET: Yes, sir!

DE LA BRIVE: And all I need to use is my wits?

MERCADET: Yes - with a certain amount of care and discretion. But you'll always remain, as the English say, on the right side of the law.

DE LA BRIVE: So what do I have to do?

MERCADET: You have to pretend to be someone rather like a rich uncle from America - a sort of friend turned up from the Indies.

DE LA BRIVE: If that's all...

MERCADET: And then you buy shares low in order to sell them high.

DE LA BRIVE: On my own say-so?

MERCADET: No, I'm still an authorised signatory. I can sign on this friend's behalf. My dear associate - for he's still my associate whether he likes it or not - made use of our mutual agreement to

	endorse the assets he stole from me back in 1830. I feel I'm fully justified in using the same tactics against him today.
DE LA BRIVE:	Indeed.
MERCADET:	Just so long as nobody recognises you - or finds out -
DE LA BRIVE:	I intend to cease to be this person just as soon as I've given you your forty seven thousand, two hundred and thirty francs and sixty-nine centimes' worth.
MERCADET:	(LISTENING) I think Justin's listening at the door. (VERY LOUD) Go in, Godeau, I beg you. Go in, please - you'll ruin me. Godeau, you're tired, have a rest -

HE PUSHES DE LA BRIVE BACK INTO THE BEDROOM. JUSTIN CALLS.

JUSTIN:	Monsieur Berchut's here.

MERCADET OPENS THE DOOR TO ADMIT BERCHUT.

MERCADET:	Good morning, Berchut. I gather there was a fall in Lower Indre mine shares yesterday.
BERCHUT:	A steep one. Monsieur Goulard turned up and sold some at twenty five per cent below what he paid for them. God knows what the panic will take them down to today.
MERCADET:	Listen - if the shares drop to fifteen per cent below yesterday's price, I'll take two thousand.

BERCHUT:	(CALCULATING IN HIS POCKET BOOK) That'll be three hundred thousand francs.
MERCADET:	That's what I'd calculated too. If they reach par again, they'll be worth six hundred thousand.
BERCHUT:	On what terms then - and how will you cover me?
MERCADET:	Cover you! Don't be absurd! Bring me the shares straight here and I'll pay for them.
BERCHUT:	Ah, I see - so you're buying on behalf of you know who -
MERCADET:	You know who?
BERCHUT:	Godeau. I know he's back.
MERCADET:	Berchut, I'm lost if everyone finds out. Who told you?
BERCHUT:	Your porter - a tip loosened his tongue.
MERCADET:	My fault for not using a piece of gold to seal it.
BERCHUT:	In any case, if you really want to keep his return quiet, I'd send his carriage back to the suppliers. Your creditors intend to bankrupt you, I gather - and if they see that, there'll be no stopping them.
MERCADET:	Oh, I think they'll hold on - if they smell ready cash at the end of the wait.
BERCHUT:	True. (ASIDE) You can never be sure with this slippery customer so it's best to show willing. (ALOUD) Tell me frankly now - are these shares being bought by Godeau?
MERCADET:	(ASIDE) Here we go!
BERCHUT:	Because if they are - all he has to do is give me a written instruction. That'll be quite enough.

MERCADET:	(ASIDE) Just what I'd hoped! (ALOUD) He's asleep at present but, as soon as he's awake, you'll have your instruction.
BERCHUT:	Agreed then. Several speculators have already commissioned me to sell off their shares at any price.
MERCADET:	And when's settlement due?
BERCHUT:	In ten days' time.
MERCADET:	Very well - send the shares over to Duval. I ashamed to admit it but Godeau's made him his banker instead of me.
BERCHUT:	(ASIDE) I don't blame him!
MERCADET:	It's a pity but what I can I say? He's so full of good intentions towards me. (SOTTOVOCE) Not a word, mind, but we're going to start up again in business. By the end of the year, we should be able to send a hundred thousand francs in commission your way.
BERCHUT:	Shall I start my account with the Lower Indre shares?
MERCADET:	(ASIDE) So now we've got another accomplice acting in good faith! (ALOUD) By all means, Berchut, but keep what you're doing as quiet as possible - use the darkest corner of the outer ring. (HANDING HIM A LETTER) Here - once you've bought, get this letter put into all the papers and let everyone know that's what you've done. Strictly in confidence, by the time the main Bourse opens, the shares should already have risen by fifteen per cent. Just remember - Godeau's

	return is secret. If anyone asks, deny it.
BERCHUT:	You can rely on me.
MERCADET:	(ASIDE) He'll shout it from the rooftops.

BERCHUT GOES OUT. MADAME MERCADET COMES IN.

MERCADET:	(ASIDE) Ah, here comes my wife. Women always spoil everything by fussing - (ALOUD) My dear, what's the matter? You look very miserable.
MADAME:	Can you wonder? You were counting on Julie's marriage to restore your credit and pacify your creditors but after yesterday's events you're completely at their mercy. Isn't there something I can do to help?
MERCADET:	(ASIDE) She'll ruin everything if she stays around. I shall have to be short with her. (ALOUD) Help! You've not been much help so far, have you? You've known Méricourt for eighteen months without finding out what he was up to. Do you know why he was so keen on this marriage? Because he's one of Michonnin's creditors. I'm afraid the only thing you're good for is keeping house. Help indeed! Well, actually, now I come to think of it - It's a lovely day. Order a magnificent calash, get dressed up in all your finery and take Julie for a drive through the Bois de Boulogne - followed by lunch at Saint Cloud. That's the most helpful thing you can do.

| MADAME: | (ASIDE) He's plotting something. I can always tell. And this time I want to know everything. |

JULIE BRINGS IN MINARD.

JULIE:	Father, it's Adolphe -
MERCADET:	Well, monsieur, are you back to ask for my daughter's hand again?
JULIE:	Yes, father, he is.
MINARD:	Julie's telling the truth, monsieur. I discussed my feelings with Monsieur Duval, who's always been like a father to me. He's seen your daughter grow up and strongly approved of my choice. He said she was just like her mother - honourable, steady and unmercenary. Encouraged, I've spoken to your daughter again - and she's graciously forgiven my shameful lapse.
MERCADET:	I'm afraid your first thoughts were better. I can't let my daughter marry a man without any fortune.
MINARD:	But, monsieur, I have a small fortune without knowing it.
MERCADET:	Aha!
MINARD:	When my mother entrusted me to Monsieur Duval's care, she left some money for my upkeep but he invested it instead. This little sum now amounts to thirty thousand francs. When I heard of your difficulties, I begged Monsieur Duval to entrust me with it. I've brought it here for you now. Maybe if you can pay off a little of what you owe then you'll gain some time and -

MADAME:	(WIPING AWAY TEARS) You're a good boy, Adolphe.
JULIE:	I'm proud of you.
MERCADET:	Thirty thousand francs! (ASIDE) I could triple that in two weeks by buying into Birotteau gas. It wouldn't be difficult to set up and... no, stop it, I mustn't. (ALOUD) My dear child, you still believe in self-sacrifice. If I could pay off debts of three hundred thousand francs with thirty thousand francs - then my fortune, France's, the world's, would be made tomorrow. So please keep your money.
MINARD:	You won't take it?
MERCADET:	(ASIDE) I think I can hold off my creditors for another month. After that, I'm made. It's tempting to borrow from Minard to keep myself going but I mustn't. It's one thing to gamble with shareholders' money, another to do it with the money of your nearest and dearest. When family's involved, you can't keep a clear head. (ALOUD) Adolphe, you shall marry my daughter -
MINARD:	Thank you, monsieur - oh, Julie -
MERCADET:	When she has a dowry of three hundred thousand francs.
MINARD:	Then we're back where we started.
MERCADET:	Not necessarily. (ASIDE) I only need to sell the two thousand shares at twenty five per cent above par... (ALOUD) It could all happen in a month, Minard, so if you wish to do me a favour - no, please keep your portfolio closed - then take my wife and daughter out. (ASIDE) Phew!

Temptation resisted! Still, even if I go under, I shall make their little capital work for them. I'll show them how to handle their funds. The main thing is that my poor daughter's loved. Dear children, they've hearts of gold both of them. I'll make them rich if it kills me. In the meantime, I must go and instruct my Godeau -

HE GOES OUT.

MINARD:	I'm glad that I've been able to make some amends for my behaviour.
MADAME:	Dear Adolphe - if nothing else, at least disaster shows you who your true friends are.
JULIE:	I won't thank you now - I've my whole life for that. But I shall always treasure this moment.
MADAME:	Ah, my dear children, if only your father wanted to settle his debts and give up business then we could all go and live in the country and be happy there. I can't tell you how much I long for honest, quiet obscurity. I'm so tired of these frantic shifts between luxury and despair.
MINARD:	Do you think you could persuade your husband?
MADAME:	I don't know. This is his life. He's like an unlucky gambler always thinking his luck will change.
JULIE:	Cheer up, mother. Maybe this time he will triumph on the Bourse.
MADAME:	It'll take more than that to change him. I can't begin to imagine how we'll ever do that. Oh dear, here

comes one of his most uncompromising creditors.

GOULARD ENTERS.

GOULARD:	Madame, forgive me for intruding. I don't wish to make a nuisance of myself but I would like to put myself at the disposal of my good friend Mercadet.
MINARD:	(TO MADAME) He seems very polite.
JULIE:	(TO MADAME) Maybe father's found some way to -
MADAME:	(ASIDE) That's what worries me. (ALOUD) He'll be back presently, Monsieur Goulard.
GOULARD:	I'm fully aware, Madame, of the happy change in your circumstances.
JULIE:	Then please tell us, monsieur, because we know nothing about it.
GOULARD:	(ASIDE) She's a sharp little thing!
MADAME:	No, tell us, please, what's happened?
GOULARD:	But you must know - he's back.
MADAME:	Who?
GOULARD:	His partner, Godeau.
MADAME:	But that's wonderful news - isn't it, Julie? (TO GOULARD) Have you seen Godeau then? Has he come back rich?
GOULARD:	You know perfectly well he came here late last night -
MADAME:	Godeau - here? Last night?
GOULARD:	I saw his coach.
JULIE:	It's true, mother, a coach did arrive last night.
MADAME:	But, monsieur, I swear to you - no one came here last night.

122

GOULARD:	If you insist, Madame. I'm sure you have your instructions from your husband.
MADAME:	Monsieur -
GOULARD:	But he won't be able to hide Godeau from us for long. We'll wait - a month if necessary. But it's all over the outer ring this morning that Godeau has taken two thousand shares in the Lower Indre mines. Not a good way to start, I'm afraid. But then I suppose if you've been away in the Indies all that time, you lose your touch a bit and you're bound to make mistakes.
MADAME:	Monsieur, I've not the least idea what you're talking about.
GOULARD:	Very well, then I'll speak plain French. Listen, Madame - if you can contrive to get me an interview with Godeau then I'm prepared to make a little reduction on the amount I'm owed.
JULIE:	Neither my mother nor I know anything about business.
GOULARD:	(ASIDE) You have to hand it to him. He really knows how to make use of his wife and family. Both of them standing there as if butter wouldn't melt in their mouths. I knew I should have married.
MADAME:	(TO GOULARD) Monsieur, I'll send my husband to you. (TO JULIE) I fear that your father's plotting something. He wants to get us out of the way. But this time I'm going to keep an eye.

SHE GOES OUT WITH JULIE.

123

GOULARD:	Listen, monsieur, I know you're marrying the daughter because Duval told me. If old man Duval advised you in favour of this marriage, it's because he knew Godeau was coming back. After all, Duval's the only one Godeau trusts. Berchut knows all about it.
MINARD:	Then Berchut knows more than me. It's you who told me Godeau had come back.
GOULARD:	Ah, I see, you're one of the family now - and part of the conspiracy of silence. Well, listen carefully, because this is in Mercadet's interests - Tell Godeau that if he's prepared to pay me on the nail, I'll give a reduction of twenty five per cent.
MINARD:	I'm afraid I've no right to involve myself in Monsieur Mercadet's affairs. He'd quite correctly take it ill if I did. Besides, here he comes now...

MERCADET ENTERS.

MERCADET:	Adolphe, the ladies are waiting. (SOFTLY) Take them out to dine in the country - or, I warn you, you'll never marry Julie.
MINARD:	I promise.

HE LEAVES.

MERCADET:	Well, Goulard, I gather my fate is sealed. You're going to force me to file for bankruptcy. I am, after all, only a failed speculator.

GOULARD:	You? One of the most capable men in Paris! A man who only needs another break to make millions!
MERCADET:	But I thought you all got together last night to -
GOULARD:	To discuss how to help you. We're prepared to wait as long as you need.
MERCADET:	If only you'd said that yesterday - but I mustn't be ungrateful.

JUSTIN ENTERS.

MERCADET:	What is it, Justin?
JUSTIN:	(SOFTLY) Monsieur - it's Monsieur Violette. He's offered me sixty francs if I let him speak to Godeau.
MERCADET:	Sixty francs! (ASIDE) He robbed me of those yesterday!
JUSTIN:	Monsieur doesn't object if I profit by this opportunity?
MERCADET:	Not at all. Let yourself be bribed. You have my permission to fleece them all.
JUSTIN:	I'll do my best, monsieur.
MERCADET:	Goulard, if you'll excuse me - Justin's brought me some news and I need to pen a short note regarding it.

HE LEAVES.

GOULARD:	I know what's going on.
JUSTIN:	Monsieur is always most perceptive.
GOULARD:	How much did Violette offer you to let him speak to Godeau?
JUSTIN:	So monsieur knows that Monsieur Godeau has... No, you're wrong, he offered me nothing.
GOULARD:	What did he offer?

JUSTIN:	You're asking me to betray Monsieur Mercadet who wants the return kept a complete secret... Two hundred francs.
GOULARD:	Here's three hundred.
JUSTIN:	(ASIDE) If only Monsieur Godeau came back every day.
GOULARD:	I must, of course, be the first to see him. I have a debt of seventy thousand francs to discuss.
JUSTIN:	If monsieur would like to wait in the small ante-room with Monsieur Violette, then I'll let him know when Monsieur Godeau takes lunch - Monsieur Mercadet has asked for him to be served in here.
GOULARD:	Excellent.

GOULARD LEAVES.

JUSTIN:	It's as easy as dropping fish into a fishpond.
MERCADET:	(ENTERING) Well?
JUSTIN:	I await monsieur's orders regarding Monsieur Godeau...
MERCADET:	For the moment, just go and collect your bribes - and, whatever you do, don't listen to what Godeau and I are saying to each other. (JUSTIN LEAVES) That guarantees he puts his ear to the door. (PAUSE) You know, it's really rather alarming just how like Godeau he looks. Or, at least, Godeau as I'd imagine him after ten years in the Indies. (CALLS) Come on out -

DE LA BRIVE ENTERS
DISGUISED AS GODEAU.

DE LA BRIVE:	My dear friend, this Parisian climate is simply frightful. If it wasn't for my son, I'd never have come back. But is high time the poor boy learned that his father's finally married his mother.
MERCADET:	(RINGING - AND TALKING UNDER THE NOISE) You make a very convincing old man - you must have done this before.
DE LA BRIVE:	I made my debut in '27 at a private theatre in Touraine. Opposite a marquise of a certain age who insisted on playing the juvenile lead.

ENTER JUSTIN.

MERCADET:	You can serve Monsieur now. Oh, and bring a light for his hookah.
JUSTIN:	Monsieur, Pierquin's downstairs trying to bribe Pere Grumeau.
MERCADET:	As soon as my wife and daughter have gone out, let him in.

JUSTIN SERVES LUNCH TO DE
LA BRIVE. MERCADET LIGHTS
THE HOOKAH.

JUSTIN:	(ASIDE) He certainly helps himself to the food like an old friend.
MERCADET:	(ASIDE) Maybe I'd better write a note to Duval to ask him to back me up. He's rather strait-laced but he is very fond of Julie so he should help me out.

HE WRITES THE NOTE THEN HANDS IT TO JUSTIN.

MERCADET: Justin - get that porter to take this note over to Monsieur Duval.

JUSTIN LEAVES.

DE LA BRIVE: (EATING) This is excellent. How are we doing?

MERCADET: It's still risky. Lower Indre shares could stay below par.

DE LA BRIVE: What happens to us if they do?

MERCADET: Bah! The chances are fifty / fifty. There's no point in worrying about it.

GOULARD AND VIOLETTE COME IN.

GOULARD: What did I tell you? He's hidden away like a private fortune.

VIOLETTE: My dear Monsieur Mercadet -

MERCADET: Please excuse me, I'm busy-

GOULARD: And we know who with.

MERCADET: I very much doubt it.

VILETTE: It's the worthy Monsieur Godeau.

MERCADET: Who spun you that fairy story? I declare to you, Pere Violette, n all honesty, that this man here is not Godeau. Goulard will bear me out.

GOULARD: (TO VIOLETTE) He's as full of lies as one of his company prospectuses. But that's how it is in business.

VIOLETTE: It wouldn't survive otherwise.

GOULARD: Despite your insistence, Mercadet, that's Godeau to the life. I recognise him - there's no point in denying it.

MERCADET: Oh very well, I won't deny that Godeau - and I want the whole of

128

	Paris to know this - that Godeau, who duped me once but who has now proved to be the honest, the good, the thoughtful, the far-sighted Godeau, is in fact due.
VIOLETTE:	We know - he's back from Calcutta.
GOULARD:	With a huge fortune -
MERCADET:	A fortune that is incalcutta - ulable.
GOULARD:	It's wonderful news. I suppose he's become what's known as a nabob.
VIOLETTE:	A nabob? So how do you address a nabob?
MERCADET:	Please leave him alone. As you can appreciate, I don't want any of my creditors bothering him.
GOULARD:	(SIDLING UP TO DE LA BRIVE) Your excellency -
MERCADET:	Goulard, please - I won't allow it.
VIOLETTE:	He's become completely Indian!
MERCADET:	He's certainly changed a great deal. The Indies have that effect on people. You know - the cholera, the curry...
GOULARD:	(AGAIN SIDLING UP) Pay what your friend Mercadet owes me and I'll give a twenty per cent reduction.
DE LA BRIVE:	Do you have the papers?
MERCADET:	Goulard, please -
GOULARD:	My dear Mercadet, he's only offering to settle your debts. Why are you so reluctant?
VIOLETTE:	(ALSO SIDLING UP) We never thought to see you again, Monsieur Godeau.

THE DOOR OPENS AND
MADAME MERCADET COMES
IN FOLLOWED BY JULIE AND
MINARD.

THE SOUND OF CREDITORS
GATHERING OUTSIDE IS
HEARD.
AN AWKWARD PAUSE AS SHE
TAKES IN THE SITUATION -
AND THE DISGUISED DE LA
BRIVE IN PARTICULAR.
SHE INDICATES TO JULIE AND
MINARD TO GO THROUGH TO
HER ROOM.

MERCADET:	My dear, what a surprise.
MADAME:	I think I understand why you didn't want me here.
MERCADET:	My dear, please -
MADAME:	No, Auguste, let me do what is right -
MERCADET:	(ASIDE) She's going to have one of her fits of uncompromising honesty and finish me off. (ALOUD) If you care for me -
MADAME:	You know I do. That's why I must speak. (TO THE CREDITORS) Messieurs, stop please.

THE CREDITORS WHO STILL
CLUSTER ROUND DE LA BRIVE
WITH THEIR PAPERS NOW
TURN TO FACE HER. SHE
GATHERS HER COURAGE.

MADAME:	I'm afraid Monsieur Mercadet has been the victim of a very poor joke - (SHE STARES AT THE DISGUISED DE LA BRIVE) - at least that's what I'd like to believe. You too are victims.
GOULARD:	But, Madame -
MADAME:	You have been deceived.

130

VIOLETTE:	I don't understand -
MADAME:	Messieurs, please - believe me. And - if you are prepared to keep quiet about an episode I'd rather not have too closely looked into - then you will be paid.
GOULARD:	And who, may I ask, is going to pay us?
MADAME:	Monsieur Duval.

THE TWO CREDITORS GO INTO A HUDDLE.

MERCADET:	(ASIDE) She's done it now. I might have guessed.
MADAME:	Go to Monsieur Duval's this evening, Messieurs. I will be there and I will ensure that all Monsieur Mercadet's creditors will be satisfied.
VIOLETTE:	(LOOKING AT GOULARD) In that case -

VIOLETTE AND GOULARD LEAVE. AS THE DOOR OPENS, THE OTHER CREDITORS ARE HEARD AGAIN. BUT THEIR VOICES NOW DIE AWAY.

DE LA BRIVE:	(RISING) You know, Madame, if you weren't a woman, I would - can't you see I'm Monsieur de la Brive.
MADAME:	Monsieur de la Brive? Oh, surely not.
DE LA BRIVE:	Allow me to know who I really am, Madame.
MERCADET:	(ASIDE) She's so forceful I hardly recognise her.
MADAME:	But, you see I had a good opportunity to form an opinion of

	Monsieur de la Brive at supper last night. He's a young man who knows there's nothing dishonourable about debt - just so long as you're prepared to work hard to pay it off. He's a young man with his whole life ahead of him and he wouldn't want to blight his future by being involved in anything against the law.
DE LA BRIVE:	Unfortunately, Madame, the fact remains that I am Monsieur de la Brive.
MADAME:	I don't want to know who you really are any more, monsieur - not after this. I just hope you appreciate that I have pulled you back from the edge of an abyss.
DE LA BRIVE:	I'm afraid it was your husband who pushed me towards the edge in the first place. He promised to give me back the letters of exchange which threaten to ruin my life.
MADAME:	Monsieur, my husband is an honest man. He will do what he's promised - the documents will be yours.
MERCADET:	Just a moment -
MADAME:	For repayment - your word will be sufficient for the moment. I am confident you will repay your debts in full later when you have earned the money by honest toil.
DE LA BRIVE:	You really mean that?
MERCADET:	I'd just like to -
MADAME:	The true road, the road of honesty, is not an easy one - but if you work hard, I don't doubt that heaven will reward your labours.
DE LA BRIVE:	Madame, I don't know what to say. I'm overwhelmed. Nobody's ever

treated me like this before. You've opened my eyes. I'll try and do as you suggest, really I will. This idea of working hard is certainly a very interesting one. I'll give it my serious consideration. In the mean time, I don't know how to thank you enough. I shall always remember you fondly for what you've done.

HE RESPECTFULLY KISSES MADAME MERCADET'S HAND AND GOES BACK INTO MERCADET'S ROOM.
A LONG PAUSE.

MERCADET: Well, Madame, you've just comprehensively ruined me. I hope you realise that if things had continued the way they were going, my bankruptcy would have vanished as if by magic. Now, on the other hand... Have you by any chance come across a gold mine - or do you have access to a personal printing press inside the Bank of France?

MADAME: I've been seeking our honour.

MERCADET: And since you've found it, is there any money attached?

MADAME: Please don't mock me, Auguste. Something told me you were going to sacrifice your integrity in order to save your fortune. Forgive me, I'm probably very naive - but I'd rather be honest than rich. I can't bear the thought of you ceasing to be the loyal, decent and brave man I love.

MERCADET:	But don't you see? It was all working so well. Now I've sunk lower than the debts of Haiti.
MADAME:	I know you'll probably dismiss this as a foolish, female idea but at least do me the courtesy of listening - I have inherited some two hundred thousand francs. Surely you can use them to satisfy your creditors? We could do it this evening at Monsieur Duval's.
MERCADET:	But what are we left with then? We'll be as destitute as Spain.
MADAME:	We'll be rich in the respect of other people.
MERCADET:	But not in anything else.
MADAME:	We can all work, can't we? - Julie, Adolphe, I myself - even you, Auguste. We can start life anew on Adolphe's small capital and we'll be able to earn enough to live in humble but tranquil honesty. I know there are thousands of ways for a speculator to make money but they're all degrading. In my opinion, there's only one decent way of making money - by honest hard work. I may be old-fashioned but for me the three essential domestic virtues are patience, wisdom and thrift. You possess a wife who loves and respects you, two children who cherish you - allow us to continue to think well of you. Leave this stifling atmosphere of lies, of double cross, of bogus wealth. So long as we have bread, we can eat heartily - and the bread won't stick in our throats like

	expensive delicacies bought with the ruin of unhappy shareholders.
MERCADET:	(ASIDE) Once you admit your wife is in the right, you lose all authority. Women always claim to be full of generous impulses but you can't rely on the generosity lasting.
MADAME:	You're hesitating...
MERCADET:	With the best of intentions, no doubt, you've destroyed all my hopes of retrieving my fortune in one fell swoop - and now you expect me to be grateful. You'll also probably ready to join in the rush to condemn me for what I've tried to do.
MADAME:	Of course not. But let me consult two young hearts which haven't yet been hardened by the ways of the world. Let's see what they think about your plan. If you'll be good enough to go back into your study for a couple of minutes.
MERCADET:	As you wish. (ASIDE) At least I'll have a chance to consider whether there's any way left out of this disaster.

HE LEAVES. JULIE AND MINARD ENTER.

MADAME:	Come in here, my children -
MINARD:	What is it, Madame?
MADAME:	Your father finds himself in a more desperate situation than I had imagined. This time, as he says himself, it's do or die. Now it would be possible for him to pay off his debts and make a fresh fortune very quickly - but it would require guile

	and nerve. The plan's risky and it would need our help because everyone has to believe that Godeau has come back. So if you, Adolphe, were able to successfully disguise yourself as him - then Monsieur Mercadet could buy shares in Godeau's name and obtain better terms from his creditors. When the shares go up, everyone will be satisfied - the shares paid for and the creditors squared. Of course, we will also need the co-operation of Monsieur Duval -
JULIE:	Mother, your love for my father is leading you astray! Forgive me but I can't believe he could make up such a plan - and if Adolphe gets involved, I won't marry him -
MINARD:	Well said, Julie. Madame, demand my life, demand everything I own - but don't ask me to get involved in this trickery. I'll go and beg Monsieur Mercadet not to go ahead. What you are asking of me, Madame, is -
MADAME:	Sharp practice?
MINARD:	Far worse than that. Even if the plan succeeded, we'd all still be dishonoured. Forgive me, Madame, but it's -
JULIE:	Don't say any more, Adolphe.
MINARD:	In the name of all you hold dearest, Madame, give up this idea. Bankruptcy is preferable. At least after that it's possible to pick yourself up and start afresh.

MERCADET RE-ENTERS.

MERCADET:	Tell me, Adolphe, would you marry the daughter of a bankrupt?
MINARD:	Yes, monsieur - because I'd work for his rehabilitation.

THE THREE OF THEM GATHER ROUND MERCADET.

MERCADET:	Very well, I'm vanquished. (TO MADAME) You are a good and noble creature. (ASIDE) How many people spend their lives looking for such a treasure? I'd be mad not to make sacrifices to hold on to her. (ALOUD) You all deserve a better future.
MADAME:	Now you are as you were before Godeau left.
MERCADET:	You mean, because I'm ruined - but honest. (PAUSE) But I am truly lost, you know, whatever you all say. There's no doubt about it. (APART - BUT TO BE HEARD) Yes, there's nothing for it now. I can't go on. There's only one thing left to do.

HE RUSHES OUT.

MADAME:	Run after your father. Make sure he doesn't do something foolish. I fear the worst.

SHE FOLLOWS AFTER MINARD AND JULIE.
A PAUSE. DE LA BRIVE COMES BACK OUT - DRESSED IN HIS OWN CLOTHES AGAIN. HE LOOKS ABOUT.

HE OPENS THE DOOR AND
LISTEN. THERE'S NO SOUND
ANYWHERE.
HE PAUSES TO PULL HIMSELF
TOGETHER AND THEN,
ALMOST JAUNTILY, HE GOES
OUT TO FACE THE WORLD.

THREE

LATER THE SAME DAY. JUSTIN ENTERS FIRST. HE INDICATES FOR VIRGINIE, WHO CARRIES HER ACCOUNT BOOKS, TO FOLLOW. JUSTIN GOES OVER TO THE DOOR, LOOKS THROUGH THE KEYHOLE AND LISTENS.

JUSTIN: Do they imagine they can hide what's going on from us?

VIRGINIE: Pere Grumeau says the master's going to be arrested. I want my accounts settled. There's all this money owed me - on top of my wages.

JUSTIN: I can't hear anything. They're talking too quietly. It's not right - they were shouting at the top of their voices earlier on.

VIRGINIE: Justin, can I ask you something? What exactly is a bankruptcy?

JUSTIN: Well, it's a sort of involuntary theft - it's perfectly legal but there are a lot of formalities you have to go through. But the word is that monsieur's going into liquidation instead.

VIRGINIE: What's that when it's at home?

JUSTIN: Well, liquidation is when you make yourself bankrupt voluntarily instead of letting your creditors do it. You avoid a lot of the complications that way.

VIRGINIE: You understand everything, Justin.

JUSTIN: I've sat at the feet of an expert.

BREDIF ENTERS UNSEEN BY
THE SERVANTS.

BREDIF: This time I'm really going to get my hands on my apartment - and not in three months' time but in two weeks'. (LOOKING ROUND) All that gilding he's had done - that'll put at least another three thousand francs on the new rent.

JUSTIN: Here's monsieur.

THE SERVANTS CONCEAL
THEMSELVES. MERCADET
ENTERS LOOKING DEPRESSED
AND SUBDUED.

MERCADET: What do you want, Monsieur Brédif? Your apartment? Take it.

BREDIF: (ASIDE) I do want to make sure he really goes this time. He has such a nasty habit of bouncing back. (ALOUD) Monsieur, you will appreciate that I have your interests at heart. Not like those creditors who've been up and down wearing my staircase out. You know that I own the house adjoining this in the Rue de Menars. At the end of my garden, there's a concealed door which leads directly into the courtyard of this other house.

MERCADET: I'm sure there is but why are you bothering to tell me this?

BREDIF: Well, if by any chance, you should want to flee -

MERCADET: Why should I want to do that?

BREDIF: They do say it's all over for you.

140

MERCADET:	(ASIDE) Here they come then - all the dreaded horrors of bankruptcy. (NOTICING HIS SERVANTS) What are you doing here? Be off with you.
JUSTIN:	We'd like nothing better, monsieur, but we're waiting -
MERCADET:	For what?
VIRGINIE:	For our wages.
MERCADET:	Go to Madame Mercadet. She will pay you.

VIRGINIE AND JUSTIN LEAVE.

MERCADET:	I on the other hand, Monsieur Brédif, have no intention of leaving.
BREDIF:	But don't you appreciate the danger of your position?
MERCADET:	I think I'm in an excellent position.
BREDIF:	(ASIDE) He's lost his head.
MERCADET:	Tell me - what will you give me to break my lease? You'll gain three thousand a year by that, won't you? Seven years times three thousand gives twenty one thousand francs. Would you consider doing a deal?
BREDIF:	(ASIDE) Damn, he's not lost his head after all! (ALOUD) But, my dear monsieur -
MERCADET:	Everything I have is up for grabs and I have done what every other bankrupt does - get all I can.
BREDIF:	But don't you realise that if you're indicted, I shall be a material witness?
MERCADET:	Witness to what?
BREDIF:	Witness to the arrival of Godeau's supposed coach here last night - empty!

MERCADET:	My wife must be right - I am going mad! Brédif, go along to the Champs Elysees - Widows' Alley -
BREDIF:	What about it?
MERCADET:	It's filled with empty coaches. One more or less won't make any difference.
BREDIF:	(ASIDE) It's obvious that his creditors are going to have their work cut out to put one over on him. (ALOUD) Your servant then.
MERCADET:	And yours.

BREDIF GOES OUT.

MERCADET:	Oh, the endless greed! But it's in the nature of things, I suppose - and the river is always thirstier than the stream. Here comes Berchut now. This is where my punishment really begins. Brédif was just the warning shot - this is where the real assault starts. I must prepare to wallow in humiliation. Good day, Berchut.

BERCHUT ENTERS.

BERCHUT:	Good day, Monsieur Mercadet.
MERCADET:	You look depressed. Haven't the Lower Indre shares gone up?
BERCHUT:	That's just it, monsieur. We'd already reached par this morning. There's been a great deal of excitement. Your letter worked wonders. The Company realised what's happening and they're finally going to release to the Bourse the result of the sounding operations. It's certainly taking off.

MERCADET:	I trust you followed my advice and bought on your own account?
BERCHUT:	Oh yes, five hundred -
MERCADET:	So, thanks to me, you've put - what? - around five hundred thousand francs in your own pocket. Enough to buy Madame Berchut a coach and horse if she wants. I hate to see a pretty woman on foot. In any case, if we're twenty five per cent above par, now's the time to sell.
BERCHUT:	(ASIDE) You've got to hand it to him. He's good to everybody - except his shareholders.
MERCADET:	Another piece of advice while I'm at it, Berchut. Get out while you can. Quit the Bourse. In the words of the Bible, those who live by the sword die by the sword.
BERCHUT:	I appreciate your advice. Unfortunately, you have some implacable enemies to deal with. (HE HOLDS UP A PIECE OF PAPER) They told me this was a forgery.
MERCADET:	A forgery? But it's written by me!
BERCHUT:	So Godeau isn't in Paris?
MERCADET:	Listen, Berchut, you're a good man. Do me a favour. Go over to Monsieur Duval's. You'll find the money you're owed for the two thousand shares there. What do you say?
BERCHUT:	If I'm paid then I'll leave this document with Monsieur Duval. I just hope for your sake that Godeau is waiting there.

MERCADET:	You're a fine fellow, Berchut! (ASIDE) That's got me out of the worst hole for now!
BERCHUT:	(ASIDE) If he's really finished, I'd rather someone other than me did the dirty deed. (ALOUD) I'll be off to Duval's then.

EXIT BERCHUT.

MERCADET:	Off you go! I'm ruined in any case. Still I'd better send Adolphe to Duval's. (HE CALLS) Adolphe! Adolphe!

MINARD ENTERS.

MERCADET:	Adolphe, run to Duval's. You know what's happened. If only Duval is prepared to satisfy Berchut then I'm saved.
MINARD:	I'll run there.

MINARD RUNS OFF.

MERCADET:	Oh no, it's too late. Here comes the enemy in force. I should have taken Brédif's offer and fled.

JUSTIN ENTERS FOLLOWED BY
VIOLETTE, GOULARD,
PIERQUIN AND VERDELIN.

MERCADET:	This is it. Goodbye, Justin, I've tried to be a good master.
JUSTIN:	(ASIDE) I don't think I'm ready to leave him just yet. (ALOUD) I'm still with Monsieur for another ten days.

MERCADET:	Has my wife finished settling the accounts?
JUSTIN:	She's having a bit of trouble with Virginie. Virginie's not of the brightest. Her sums never add up properly.
MERCADET:	I know the feeling.
JUSTIN:	(ASIDE - AS HE RETIRES) You've got to hand it to the master. He always keeps his sense of humour.
VIOLETTE:	Monsieur -
MERCADET:	Well, Pere Violette, what can I do for you? Everything falls apart in the end, doesn't it? Still, I won't be the first to go this way.
VIOLETTE:	Oh, don't say that. Men like you are rare. If only you'd had sons! I mean, to have settled everything - the fees, the interest, all of it -with that huge ruby gleaming on his finger. Forgive me but I really didn't believe Godeau had returned.
MERCADET:	What did you say? Is this some sort of joke?
GOULARD:	My friend, I misjudged you. It's magnificent!
MERCADET:	They've obviously all decided to get their own back on me.
PIERQUIN:	I don't believe in making speeches but I will say one thing - it's turned out well after all.
VERDELIN:	It's a privilege to be your friend. We're proud of you.
PIERQUIN:	It's a pleasure to do business with you.
VIOLETTE:	Please hold on to my money -
GOULARD:	You really are a most honourable man! Paid in full! When we'd all

	have been prepared to take a reduction.
PIERQUIN:	Honourable! He's a hero!
VIOLETTE:	A true gentleman!
MERCADET:	So, messieurs, have you all had your amusement? Go on, laugh your fill. I've never minded people having a joke. In fact, I'm glad you're all here - because I've come to a momentous decision. I want to make an announcement. It's a very simple one. If you don't give me time to pay - then I shall cut my throat here and now - before your very eyes...

HE PULLS OUT A RAZOR.

MERCADET:	You don't believe I would, do you?
VERDELIN:	There's no need for these threats.
MERCADET:	I've said I'll do it - and I will.
VERDELIN:	But we've all been paid by Godeau.
MERCADET:	Godeau? But don't you understand? Godeau's a myth - a phantom. He's never going to come back. You all know that perfectly well.
ALL:	But he's here.
MERCADET:	Back from Calcutta?
ALL:	Yes!
GOULARD:	With that incalcutta-ulable fortune you joked about.
MERCADET:	I'm a desperate man. It's cruel to mock me in this way.

BERCHUT ENTERS.

BERCHUT:	Forgive me for ever doubting you, monsieur. Here are your shares. They're paid for.
MERCADET:	By whom?

BERCHUT:	By Godeau, of course.
MERCADET:	Berchut, not you as well. Not when I've made you -
BERCHUT:	A hundred and fifty thousand francs. Your plan's worked!
MERCADET:	Just a moment - you saw Godeau?
BERCHUT:	Yes - and he told me these shares were yours.
MERCADET:	Godeau did?
BERCHUT:	Who else? He's just arrived from Le Havre.

BREDIF ENTERS.

BREDIF:	Here are all the receipts, monsieur. It seems I won't be getting my apartment after all.
MERCADET:	I'm in a dream. I think I must be going crazy -

MINARD ENTERS.

MERCADET:	Adolphe, don't you try and deceive me too. All this talk about Godeau -
MINARD:	But it's perfectly true. My father is in Paris. And you were right - he has married my mother. He's recognised me as his legitimate son. I'm to be known henceforth as Adolphe Godeau.
MERCADET:	And he's really paid all these men?
MINARD:	All of them - in full. And he's paid Berchut too - because he wants you to have those shares as an advance payment on your part of what he's made in the Indies.
MERCADET:	I always said Godeau was an honest, kind-hearted, generous man - I always knew he'd come back.

Welcome, unlooked for riches - fresh from the Indies! (TO MINARD) Go and get my wife and daughter.

HE PUSHES MINARD OFF TO FETCH THEM.

MERCADET: Messieurs, I don't know what to say.
BERCHUT: I shall look forward to your future custom.
MERCADET: Oh no, Berchut. No more speculation.
VERDELIN: We should leave you alone with your family. As for the three thousand francs, keep them to buy Julie some diamond earrings.
MERCADET: (ASIDE) He's so generous I hardly know him.

THE CREDITORS LEAVE WITH JUSTIN. MINARD RETURNS WITH MADAME MERCADET AND JULIE.

JULIE: Oh, father, Adolphe has been wonderful. He's going to be a millionaire - and yet he still wants to marry me. I don't know whether to laugh or to -
MERCADET: Don't hesitate - do it.

MADAME MERCADET AND JULIE BOTH START TO CRY.

MERCADET: (TO HIS WIFE) You were so brave in adversity.
MADAME: But this makes me feel weak. Seeing you rescued - and rich.

MERCADET:	Rich - but this time honest. Come here, all of you. I have to tell you - I really couldn't cope any more. I was worn down by worry - living on my nerves all the time - never relaxed. I came very close to... well, let's not think about it.
MINARD:	My father has just bought an estate in Touraine. Why don't you become his neighbour? Be like him - put some of your money into land.
MADAME:	Ah yes, the country...
MERCADET:	Whatever you want, my dear.
MADAME:	But you'll get bored there.
MERCADET:	No... not at all. I'm sure agriculture can be fascinating. It's just a matter of learning.
MADAME:	You're sure?
MERCADET:	Yes, of course. Absolutely sure. I -

HE SWIFTLY RINGS FOR JUSTIN
BEFORE HE HAS TO SAY MORE.

| JUSTIN: | (ENTERING) Yes, monsieur ? |
| MERCADET: | Order us a cab. I've made so much use of Godeau, it's time I went and saw him in the flesh. |

HE LOOKS AT HIS FAMILY.

| MERCADET: | Come on, my dears. Let us not keep Godeau waiting. |

THEY ALL GO OUT.

END OF PLAY

www.ingramcontent.com/pod-product-compliance
Lightning Source LLC
Chambersburg PA
CBHW030519260626
47157CB00005B/1814